Strange Lights at Midnight

by

Allison Mitcham

DREAMCATCHER PUBLISHING
Saint John • New Brunswick • Canada

Canadian Cataloguing in Publication Data

Mitcham, Allison - 1932

Strange Lights at Midnight

ISBN - 1-894372-13-1
               1. Fundy, Bay of - Fiction. I. Title.
    PS8576.I86S78 2003   C813'.54   C2002-902999-6
    PR9199.3.M495S78 2003

Editor: Yvonne Wilson

Typesetter: Chas Goguen

Cover Art: Peter Mitcham

Cover Design: Dawn Drew, INK Graphic Design Services Corp.

Printed and bound in Canada

DREAMCATCHER PUBLISHING INC.
1 Market Square
Suite 306 Dockside
Saint John, New Brunswick, Canada E2L 4Z6
www.dreamcatcher.nb.ca

For Stephanie

Acknowledgements

First of all, I wish to thank my daughter Stephanie for insisting I write this book, advising me on a good many particulars pertaining to the story and accompanying me (together with her black Labrador Inkster) on numerous 'islanding' ventures. Without her support this book would not have been written.

As well, I want to thank my husband Peter for his beautiful cover picture; and the staff of DreamCatcher Publishing – particularly Elizabeth Margaris and Yvonne Wilson – for their warm-hearted and generous enthusiasm for my writing. Yvonne also deserves additional thanks for going through the manuscript with a fine tooth comb and correcting errors I had made.

Other Works by Allison Mitcham

Strange Lights at Midnight, a novel, DreamCatcher Publishing, 2003.

A Little Boy Catches a Whale, children's book, 2002. Adaptation of the Mi'kmaq (Indian) tale from Silas Rand's transcription. The book has translations in French and Mi'kmaq and watercolor illustrations opposite every story page by the author's daughter, Naomi. Published by Bouton d'or.

Angels in the Snow, a novel, Crane Creek (USA), 2000.

Maritime Voices, a collection of short stories including one of Mitcham's, co-edited with Dr. Theresia Quigley, DreamCatcher Publishing, 2000.

Meat Goats, (with Stephanie Mitcham, D.V.M.), Crane Creek Publications, 2000.

Poetic Voices of the Maritimes: a Selection of Contemporary Poetry, (co-edited with Theresia Quigley) Lancelot Press, 1996.

Taku, Heart of North America's Last Great Wilderness, illustrated by Naomi and Peter Mitcham, Lancelot Press, 1993.

Grey Owl's Favorite Wilderness Revisited, Penumbra, 1991. (Distributed by University of Toronto Press and subsequently by General Publishing.)

Atlin, the Last Utopia: subarctic outpost and portal to the land of eagle, wolf and grizzly (non-fiction study of the outpost mentality), illustrated by Naomi Mitcham, Lancelot Press, 1989. (Second printing, 1992; third printing, 1994.)

Island Keepers (biography and non-fiction study of the outpost mentality), Lancelot Press, 1989. (Second printing, 1990; third printing, 1993.)

Paradise or Purgatory: island life in Nova Scotia and New Brunswick (non-fiction study of the outpost mentality and regional folklore), Lancelot Press, 1986, (Second printing, 1987; third printing, 1994.) Illustrated by Peter Mitcham.

Numerous articles and poems in magazines, periodicals, and books.

-1-

It was impossible to imagine trouble on such a day, which just goes to show how, instinctively, most of us seem to equate fine weather with clear sailing. I learned the hard way that it's a mistake to let down your guard - ever - when you venture into potentially dangerous waters. It's also a mistake to forget the old saying that history tends to repeat itself.

As it was, at the back of my mind I'd filed all the stories Uncle Vernon had told me about the nefarious goings on on these islands over a span of two centuries. For me, these tales of smuggling, kidnapping and strange lights at midnight fit the category of folklore: delightful to hear about, hard to believe. In the two years since I'd come to live opposite these islands I'd never seen or heard tell of anything suspicious - any more than I had near my childhood home across from the Tuskets, where again there were stories galore floating around about the notorious past. Maritimers like to look backward - perhaps too much, I used to think when I was growing up.

As I busied myself for the crossing, I was thinking about practical details, not stories - trying to remember all the things Vernon had told me about the tides, together with everything my own father and brothers do when they move our sheep onto the Tusket Islands in the spring. The two places are a lot alike, except that the tides here in Passamaquoddy Bay are much higher than where I grew up.

The world's highest tides occur in offshoots of the Bay of Fundy where the water is funnelled into subsidiary bays and basins. Though Passamaquoddy Bay is one of these, even here the tides are less extreme than in the Basins of Minas and Cumberland, Fundy's farthest reaches.

Moving sheep to a Passamaquoddy island, however, poses mostly the same problems as taking them out to the Tuskets. In fact, it was partly the similarity between the two places which lured me here in the first place. There are even reckoned to be 365 islands in each group, one for every day of the year, the old-timers say. Fishing, sheep and islands are my own folks' as well as my uncle's family's common heritage.

Both the Tuskets and the Passamaquoddy Islands are, to my way of thinking, enchanted isles. Though familiar and near at hand, I find the Passamaquoddy islands as bewitching as Herman Melville and Darwin found the exotic *Encantadas*, the Galapagos. Even famous people - Franklin D. Roosevelt, for one - have felt the lure of these islands. When he could have chosen any spot in the world, Roosevelt opted to build his lovely summer home on one of them - Campobello - and sail amongst the others as long as he could.

*   *   *

But to get back to the specifics of my story, my cousin Jim has been away on business a lot over the last few years, which is why the job of taking the sheep across to their summer pasturage has fallen to my lot. Since, as I've said, I've always known about fishing boats and sheep, I feel confident most of the time.

Besides, after opting out of a university career when I finished graduate school, I feel I have to make this enterprise work. My parents sank a lot of money into my education and I'm afraid they're disappointed that I'm not using it. Well, not using it directly. Nothing you study or learn is ever really a loss. But try telling my parents that.

They decreed that I, the family's only girl, would get the expensive education. They provided my brothers with fishing boats and licences instead. Having been coached for the fishery - and some subsidiary farming and wood-cutting - from as far back as they could remember, they hadn't demonstrated any significant academic aptitudes anyway. But what my parents had never dreamed of was that I would one day decide to raise sheep.

When I told them, my father said right away: "Not with my blessing. You're not gonna follow up such a damn fool idea 'round here. No daughter of mine's gonna farm on her own."

Fortunately, though, my father's brother, my Uncle Vernon, who is more easygoing and open-minded than my father, said he'd back me, said to come right along up to Passamaquoddy Bay. Said too that he really needed help now that his son Jim spent most of his time on his computer business and had no interest anyway in farming or in the boat. So that's how I came to this place. I've never looked back.

-2-

The few clouds in the blue sky appeared merely decorative, the haze on the horizon temporary. It seemed a perfect day for delivering some of the sheep to the island, which at the moment was barely visible, just a faint smudge on the horizon. But the haze would lift: Uncle Vernon said that was a sure thing on a day like this.

The motor chugged away evenly after its recent tuneup and only a small amount of salt spray entered the boat as the occasional larger-than-average wave smacked against the wooden hull. Vernon kept procrastinating about getting a new boat - a fiberglass one - since it was clear that his only son's focus was more on computers than fishing and raising sheep, and he still wasn't totally convinced that a "slip of a girl," as he referred to me, could take over these hitherto wholly masculine enterprises. The old boat, though, is not so bad. It does have some quite modern technology - the Loran-C, for instance. I always wonder how the old-timers used to get through the sudden dense fogs so typical of this coast without one.

The ewes, ready for their freedom after an exceptionally long and chilly winter on the mainland, were handling the voyage like old seafarers, and, in fact, Spotty Dotty, a large, bossy troublemaker, was contentedly chewing her cud. The lambs were somewhat more apprehensive, this being their first boat ride, and there were occasional calls for momentarily misplaced mothers.

I planned to spend the day - the twelve hours between high tides - on the island doing odds and ends: clearing debris and brush from around the fresh water spring that provides the sheep with good drinking water, putting the salt and mineral mix out and walking the beaches and the nearby woods to check for objects that had been washed ashore in winter storms and might entrap an unwary sheep. Last year, a ewe - Charlie's Sister - fractured a leg that she somehow got stuck in a decaying lobster trap. I also hoped to have time to enjoy my lunch as well as the solitude and beauty of the island.

This island has been in Uncle Vernon's family since before the border disputes during the war of 1812 to 1814. These arguments over whether the islands in this bay belonged to Maine or New Brunswick almost turned into another war long after nearly every other altercation had been amicably settled. The contentiousness was like a family feud because nearly all the owners of these islands were related. Many of those living on the New Brunswick side were New Englanders who had fled to Canada at the time of the American Revolution. And on the American side they were, of course, still Yankees.

Vernon had told me all the ins and outs of these complicated border conflicts, ending up with their legal resolution in 1842. The way he had the facts at his fingertips, you'd think the events had all occurred yesterday.

With Daniel Webster negotiating on behalf of the Americans and Lord Ashburton, briefed by Saint John lawyer Moses Perley, defending the British Colonial claims, the Americans, he said, had driven too hard a bargain. They got all the western side of the Saint John River, which meant that lots of New Brunswick families became Americans overnight. Still, New Brunswick kept the Passamaquoddy islands. Moses Perley prodded Lord Ashburton into sticking to his guns on that one. Some Americans who couldn't bear to part with their islands did not want to become New Brunswickers, so they kept their American citizenship, bought back their islands - land cost next to nothing in those days - and kept on living as they always had. A peculiar situation, to say the least.

The only safe place to land on our island - Sheep Island, the locals call it, though its real name is Jaffray, after its first owner - is a small cove on the southeast. The rest of the island is ringed by rocks, strewn helter skelter. Many of them lurk just underwater - *sunkers*, my Cape Breton grandfather would have called them. Over the years these treacherous hidden obstacles to going ashore have holed the hulls of all kinds of vessels, particularly in fog and during bad blows. But even if it weren't for the rocks, the high, forbidding cliffs would discourage any seasoned mariner from landing elsewhere.

The island, which is roughly two miles long and a quarter of a mile wide, lies with its long portion against the mainland. The north and west sides are densely thicketed. The eastern and southern parts were cleared at one time, but some moderately large trees - spruce, birch and poplar mostly - have grown up on the fringes of the areas the sheep graze. The original white pine forests, which so impressed the early explorers, have not reappeared.

When I first came here to help out Uncle Vernon and Jim, a lot of scrub - alders, pincherries, blackberry and raspberry bushes - had begun to take over the former pastures because, for a good many years previous, Jim and Vernon had brought only a very few head of sheep over to graze. Jim lost interest in raising sheep, sharing the general view in these parts that sheep farming is a thing of the past, scarcely a break-even proposition.

But I've been determined to make a go of it, and I'm up to almost a hundred head. With the infusion of that hardy and prolific Romanov strain, I've been expanding and strengthening the herd every year. Prices are improving a bit, so I'm optimistic that the future will be rosy.

I was roused from my dreams of ewes raising four lambs a year, and these lambs bringing exceptionally high prices, by the proximity of the island. I entered the rock-free channel leading to the landing cove which you'd hardly know was there if you weren't familiar with the island: it's so sheltered by spruces which have somehow found a footing on thin patches of soil in the hollows between rocks.

The cove is enchanting, a secret place which is protected in all weathers. What also makes it remarkable is that, at high tide, the channel is deep almost up to the shore and is skirted on one side by a gravel bar which is perfect for landing sheep - or any other cargo I suppose. Our boat doesn't draw much water, but, in the old days, mariners must have been able to get a good-sized sailing vessel in here. But not for long: you only have half an hour at most to load or unload. After that the channel drains so fast that your boat is almost high and dry in the gully before you know what has happened.

If you time everything right, you can anchor the boat alongside the bar and turf the sheep out on planks at the stern shortly after the turn of the tide. They walk right out onto firmly-packed gravel and start wending their way up the beach to the pastures.

*   *   *

That first day of the season I arrived too early for everything to be ideal, but it didn't really matter: there were only about three or four inches of water covering the bar and it was clear that Spotty Dotty and her crew weren't going to be put off by such a miniscule amount. As soon as I anchored, that opinionated ewe was already agitating to get onto dry land, and Jen, my best border collie, couldn't wait to herd the whole group ashore. Jen's always keen to work, but I knew she wouldn't like those few inches of icy water. She's different in every way from Inkerman, my Labrador retriever, who'd be in his element in this situation - except for the sheep, of course. He's leery of sheep and he's hopeless at herding.

I figured I'd have to make about four trips over the ensuing week to get all the sheep onto the island. I never feel comfortable ferrying more than twenty or twenty-five at once, and I'm always careful to take an experienced sea-going ewe like Spotty Dotty on each voyage. With Jen to keep them in line that's probably not necessary, but I tend to be cautious.

One day at a time, I thought. I was determined not to think about the rest of the week, but simply enjoy this trip and the twelve hour enforced respite on the island between high tides.

-3-

Jen and I left the sheep grazing around the foundations of the old house and barn. By late next month, I noted, mentally taking stock, the lilac bushes and the apple blossoms would be out.

The pioneers, I thought as I often had before, chose such picturesque sites - this one overlooking the cove, but sheltered in a hollow, with the orchard stretching up the hillside behind it; rosebushes, blue flags, lilies-of-the-valley, tiger lilies and lilacs, planted, and still growing, near the dooryard. None of this was visible from the sea. I suppose the original settlers feared pirates and privateers. I wondered idly if any ever came ashore here in the old days: if there was ever any serious trouble on this seemingly idyllic island.

I walked towards the cliffs on the opposite side of the island, Jen close on my heels. Winter storms often wash up all sorts of fascinating objects onto the shrubs and rocks on the cliffside and onto the crescent beach which is exposed at low tide. This beach, like all Sheep Island's beaches - apart from the sandy one which rings the cove - is cut off at high tide, cut off from the adjoining beaches and from the path. It is *not* the place to be when the tide is coming in. But with the tide receding, it would be safe for hours.

As Jen and I prepared to climb down the rocky path, I noticed a cigarette pack at the base of a stunted spruce. My immediate thought was that it had been dropped by someone who had come for a picnic or perhaps to camp out overnight. Then I realized that it was too early in the season - and too cold - for casual visitors.

The package was quite new, hardly scuffed at all, so it could not have been dropped last fall. Hunters occasionally come here in October for duck hunting, but only rarely - by mistake - because they can't get off when they wish. Fishermen, for the same reason, never frequent this island. There are plenty of other islands nearby which better suit their purposes.

The brand of these cigarettes - Belvedere - was one you see in the stores every day. But, since I'm not a smoker, I soon forgot about the pack. In fact, I only picked it up and put it in my pocket because I don't like litter.

A plump seal was lying on a flat offshore rock, and, when I looked more carefully, I could see several sleek heads bobbing in the water around the rock. I'm fond of seals: they remind me of Inkerman. I know, though, that fishermen don't find them as endearing as I do.

As I looked up and down the beach and then beneath me to the lower part of the cliff, I could see that there was some cleaning up to do. Driftwood was plentiful and there were several colorful floats and buoys as well as a ragged net in which great bunches of dulse and other seaweeds were enmeshed. Since the sheep sometimes eat the seaweed, the net looked to me like a possible death trap - certainly a hazard. I decided to burn it along with a sea and rock-damaged lobster trap and some coils of rope.

While the pile was ablaze, Jen and I checked all the shoreline which we could reach. She was interested in herding the young gulls, which were brown-flecked and awkward - seemingly overweight in comparison with their sleek, white, quick-moving parents. "That'll do,

Jen," I said, not wanting them disturbed. She is more obedient than Inkerman in a situation like this - well, truth to tell, in almost any situation.

By the time the fire burned down enough so that it was safe to leave, I was so hot I decided to head for the fresh water spring. It was bubbling away as usual. After splashing the icy water on my face and having a long drink, I cleared the debris from around the sides of the cask which fills the depression. The bottom has been cut out so the water seeps up into the barrel, spills over the side and runs away towards the cliff face. It's a pretty impressive arrangement really.

The sheep prefer to drink from the overflow rather than from the barrel, so that suits everyone. Otherwise, I wouldn't feel right about drinking from the cask.

As I relaxed for a few minutes by the spring, I had the sensation that someone was watching me. I am not easily scared, and told myself not to be silly. Finding that cigarette pack must have unnerved me, I thought - more than I would have expected.

Jen seemed unconcerned, so I doubted that anyone or anything lurked in the bushes. Just the same, I decided that I would feel much more secure on the other side of the island where I could see the boat and where the pastures gave one a clear view. Not that I could get off the island, whatever happened, until the next high tide.

Now I wished that Inkerman were here: his Labrador nose would smell out an intruder. Then, I'd know for certain. With Jen I couldn't tell. Her focus is almost wholly on sheep and on my commands. At home, she tends not to react at all when a stranger comes into the farmyard, whereas Inkerman bristles and barks. He isn't a ferocious animal, but he can look terrifying when his hackles are up. I am not altogether sorry that strangers are wary of him.

On reaching the other shore, I forgot all about intruders. Spotty Dotty was standing on her hind legs, reaching up into the tree where I had carefully hung my knapsack. I couldn't believe it! Despite all the lush new pasture, the wretched animal was trying to get at my lunch.

Promising myself, as I did at least three or four times a year, that I would get rid of that ewe and all her troublesome offspring, I raced towards my lunch. As I got closer, Spotty realized that I was coming and calmly walked away, with what looked like one of my egg salad sandwiches dangling from her mouth.

When I arrived at the disaster site I was so out of breath I was ready to collapse. My apple had two big bites out of it and one of my packs of sandwiches was gone. Momentarily I hoped that the waxed paper would give that ewe severe indigestion, but of course she's far too intelligent to eat anything like that. I still had an orange, a pack of sandwiches, milk and some fruitcake left, so I was relieved that I wouldn't be obliged to go hungry all day. Jen's dog food was untouched, so that was a lucky thing too.

Having caught my breath after my sprint, I picked up the remaining contents of my knapsack and walked towards the cove beach. No matter what happened, I was going to enjoy my lunch - or what was left of it.

After lunch, I decided, I would walk along this near shore. The beach would be exposed by then and the water gone from the caves. This part of the shore frightens me a little, so I always have to psych myself up before going there.

-4-

This beach is shale and consequently slippery when it's wet. Still, it's on such a slope that nearly all the tidewater runs off at once, which means that on a sunny day it dries more quickly than most beaches. Also, unlike the beaches on the opposite side of the island, there are few hollows and consequently few tidal pools.

I picked my way slowly across the grey-blue slabs, admiring the varnish-like sheen on the rocks which hadn't dried yet. When it's wet, it's not the sort of place you'd want to be in a hurry to leave. Maybe that's one of the reasons this beach frightens me somewhat. I said to Jim once when I was first here, "What if a person slipped on the shale and broke a leg or even sprained an ankle when the tide is on its way in?"

Jim just laughed. "What if you tripped crossing the street and the traffic kept coming?" he countered. "Every place has dangerous possibilities. This is not really a scary place."

For him, no; for me, yes. The disquieting feeling I experience here is something that words cannot dispel. I've decided since that first visit, now that I've seen a lot of this shore, that my unease in this place is simply a reaction to a primeval quality with which this coast and many other parts of the Fundy coast are endowed. Strange fossilized remains of plants and creatures long since extinct, and massive copper-colored tree trunks, protrude from veins of coal. You can study the layers - all clearly laid out - as you walk along the beach.

The caves, which are exposed only at low tide, also worry me somewhat because you can't see into them. Perhaps, deep down, I expect some prehistoric creature, contemporary relatives of those etched in the rock, to emerge suddenly from one of them. The feeling is worse when fog or mist hangs over the island and its nearby islet where the cormorants - shags, in local parlance - nest. These strange-looking long-necked black sea birds are straight out of ancient times. What's more, their droppings kill the trees wherever they establish a colony, so on Shag Islet, as we call this tiny isle, only the tree skeletons remain, blackened as if by fire.

On a fine day, I'm not usually so leery of this place, yet, as I approached the first cave, I was apprehensive. Jen obviously did not share my forebodings. She darted left and right, seeming carefree and unconcerned. Her work done for the day, she appeared delighted to be able to take full advantage of her freedom. She acted like the two year old she is.

Again I wished for Inkerman's more mature presence: if he were only here, I told myself again, I'd know if there were anything to be concerned about. The odd feeling I'd had at the spring, the conviction that I was being watched - combined with finding the nearly-new cigarette package - had tainted the day.

I walked as quickly as I could past the first cave entrance - a dark hole - but saw nothing which the sheep might get caught in. The next two were the same. One more to go and then I could turn around.

The mouth of the fourth cave looked at first glance like the others - just a black hole - and I made a mental note that I had better bring a flashlight when I returned to the island. A sheep might venture through any of the cave apertures and come a cropper on something I could not see.

Jen vanished inside this one and I walked closer, calling out, "That'll do, Jen." I stood under the natural *porte cochère* waiting for her to emerge. Almost at once she reappeared beside me, unperturbed, and obedient as usual. I was turning away into the sunlight when I noticed something glistening above my head. By standing on my tiptoes I could almost reach it. But I could tell at once what it was - a rope. And squinting at it in the semi-darkness I thought, "a new rope."

It was obviously still wet from the receding tide which must have covered it. That accounted for the glistening effect which had first caught my attention. It was just ordinary rope, the kind we use on the boats when we tie up.

I thought it might perhaps be hung up on something. Next time, I told myself, I'd bring a bait box from the boat to stand on so that I could reach it down - and a flashlight, of course, to see what I was doing. If there was a long length of rope, it was worth salvaging before the sea dislodged it and one of the animals became entangled.

As I turned back towards the cove, I was still thinking about the rope. It had appeared to be hanging clear, seemingly attached above. Again my intuitive feeling that something was amiss on the island surfaced: someone could have fixed it there. But if so, for what purpose?

I began conjecturing in the way that drives my brother Perley crazy. Supposing, I thought, there was a stick of dynamite attached to that rope. When I was in school, I'd heard of rock hounds blowing up sections of the Joggins cliffs to get at the fossils. Now that such dynamiters were treated like criminals, they might, I thought, have retreated to less publicized and consequently less frequented spots on the Fundy coast.

But the more I turned this idea over in my mind, the readier I was to admit that my conjectures seemed far-fetched. Fossils could be found here certainly, but not such beauties and not in such quantities as in the now internationally famous cliffs and on the beaches at Joggins and Parrsboro. No, I told myself, if anyone was indeed up to something here, rockhounding was probably not their objective. Anyway, I promised myself that on my next visit I'd bring along flashlight, baitbox - and Inkerman.

-5-

I loaded more sheep for the island the following day. Since the morning, unlike its predecessor, was grey and raw, the prospect of a trip across the bay was not pleasant. The sky was pewter; the sea its reflection. Rain threatened, but had not yet begun. The water, however, though not dead calm, was not rough, and the visibility was adequate. Those two factors determined my going.

In the spring along the Fundy coast, you don't wait for clear skies and calm seas before you make your move. If you did, you might be waiting a long time - particularly when you need the right conjunction of tides and wind. Fine spring days are rare. The best time of year here is late summer and fall. That's when you can have one glorious day after another. Even then, nothing is certain.

I hoped to get over to Sheep Island and back before the change of the tide. If I could unload my cargo quickly and smoothly, I might be able to do it. After my careful search the preceding day, there was no need to scout the beaches so soon again. My foray into the fourth cave could wait too - probably until I'd ferried across the final load. If the weather cooperated, that would be the end of the week.

The only hitch I could imagine was getting the salt and mineral mix ashore and the feeders filled in time. It was, I thought, stupid of me to have forgotten the two bags yesterday when I'd had lots of time. It was crucial to make sure the sheep had access to the mineral mix in case the weather didn't hold and I was prevented from going to the island later in the week.

Despite the dismal weather, I was in good spirits. My apprehensions had all but vanished. They'd been allayed by a short visit Uncle Vernon and Aunt Martha had paid me. They had brought along one of Martha's seafood casseroles and half a dozen of her fresh-from-the-oven rolls - both great morale boosters.

When I'd mentioned the dangling rope in the cave, I could see that they thought my imagination had gotten out of hand. With his pipe clamped between his molars, and puffing regularly, Vernon explained how easily new rope and old got caught up on rocks and snags along this coast. Small wonder, he'd said, that the powerful tide, swirling into the cave with a load of debris, had flung some of it high into the 'rafters' of this confined space and in its sudden retreat left some behind.

"When the tide goes out of these bays and basins at the head of the Bay," he'd said, "it's like pulling the plug on a giant bathtub which has a first class drain. And there's always a spectacular ring left at the high water mark."

"My dear," he'd concluded, his slate blue eyes clear and smiling, the lines around his eyes and mouth deepening into the channels made by a lifetime of pleasant expressions, "one day you'll get used to the height and power of our tides. In your home waters - among the Tuskets - they're not even half this height. Small wonder you think someone hung things up on the rocks. Quite understandable." Vernon smiled again and puffed. I felt my concerns about the island ebbing.

Vernon is a very nice man. A kind and thoughtful man. He is also straightforward and knowledgeable about these waters as only fishermen are.

I like fishermen as a race. Sooner or later most of them have close calls, and somehow the proximity they have felt to death makes them seem more contented with their lot than other people and more tolerant of the follies and foibles of the rest of us. I find too that they're not smug about the knowledge they've accumulated, even though, when you tap into it, you find it tends to be more exact than the accredited experts'.

Vernon's puffing reminded me of the cigarette pack I'd picked up on the far side of the island. In cataloguing the previous day's events, I hadn't mentioned this pack or the eerie feeling I'd had of being watched while I was washing and drinking at the spring.

The cigarettes were still in my jacket pocket and the jacket was draped across the kitchen chair where I'd left it. I reached over and pulled out the packet. Handing it to Vernon, I told him precisely where I'd found it.

He frowned and said nothing as he turned the pack over in his calloused hands. Hands, I thought as I waited, show age more accurately than faces. The brown blotches - age spots - the network of lines, appear whether you've used your hands or saved them. And there seems to be no cosmetic 'hand-lift' that will smooth them out the way a face-lift rejuvenates some people.

Vernon interrupted my reverie by clearing his throat. It was one of his mannerisms, signaling his readiness to speak. Having spent so much time alone on his boat, I suppose that verbal communications - even with family - called for a special effort on his part. He was as economical with words as he was with everything else, seeming to calculate in advance the number he would need to use as accurately as he would pounds of bait. "Well," he remarked thoughtfully, "these smokes are what a lot of people around here buy - on both sides of the line, so the brand's not going to identify whoever left them on the island, if that's what you're thinking.

"But," he went on, emitting four or five puffs in quick succession, "I do think it's strange to find a pack - a new one like this - on the far side of Sheep Island, especially at this time of year. No one could get over to that side and back 'tween tides - and anyone local knows better 'n to try to put ashore at Sheep Island 'less it be an emergency and the tide just right to take them into the cove.... So, I agree with you. It's some strange.

"Still," he continued after a pause filled with more puffs, "I s'pose there's some good enough reason. Don't you fret, my dear, that island's a good place. As you know, I'm seventy-four, just past, and in all those years I've never heard of anything untoward happening there. The bad things all occurred long, long ago - and who knows whether those strange, old tales have any truth in them. Probably not. I shouldn't have filled your pretty head with an old man's ramblings about times before he was born. It's the memory of them that got you worried. Forget about them."

-6-

I reached the island early and anchored offshore to await the turn of the tide. The sheep remained bunched and quiet, thanks to Jen. The way she stared them down, transfixing them so that they dared not budge, has always seemed a miracle to me. Inkerman, bored as usual with the sheep, turned his attention to the cormorants. I followed his gaze, wondering idly once more why so many birds on Shag Islet had crowded into such a small space, why they packed their sinuous dark bodies so close to one another instead of spreading out onto Sheep Island. Of course I'm thankful they haven't.

My eyes shifted from the blackened trees of Shag Islet to the healthy dark green spruces and firs atop the cliffs of the main island. In another few weeks, I speculated, the poplars and birches in the interior should be showing the first of their bright new green, and, interspersed with them, the pincherries and crabapple trees would be decked out in white and pale pink blossoms. The landscape would look more cheerful then. At present, apart from the grass, only the alders and tamaracks, which were touched with a faint greenish haze, showed signs of life.

I glanced back towards the caves. Water was ebbing quickly from them. I smiled, thinking of the appropriateness of Vernon's quip about how fast they drained - "as if a plug had been pulled." As soon as the cave mouths were clear, I could move into the cove and land my cargo. The caves emptied out at roughly the same time as the small causeway in the cove was exposed. Another few minutes should do it.

And then, out of the fourth cave skimmed a Zodiac - one of those inflatable and supposedly unsinkable craft the Mounties and coast guard on the Pacific coast, not ours, are said to swear by. Propelled by a high-powered jet engine, it cleared the sunkers and shot off behind Shag Islet, disappearing so fast around Sheep Island that I could hardly believe I'd seen it. It had ridden out on the last couple of feet of water. A moment or two more and it couldn't have budged.

The man in it may have seen me, though he gave no sign that he had. Strange! Though I suppose it was possible that he'd been so focused on getting out of the cave before he was stranded there - not to mention clearing the sunkers once he'd escaped - that he'd never looked my way. If he had, he'd only have glimpsed my boat, as I had his.

I had been too surprised to wave. It seemed incomprehensible that anyone could have gotten himself into such a tight position. And then, I asked myself: when had the Zodiac come in? Not since I'd been anchored here, certainly. And not long before that the cave entrance had been blocked by a wall of water. Entering it then was a physical impossibility.... Yet there had to be an answer. Though not one I could imagine.

Meanwhile I had no time to speculate. The cave mouth was now fully agape, its shale lip already visible; so the causeway in the cove must be exposed. It was time to land my sheep.

The causeway was altogether clear by the time I anchored alongside and, with Jen's help, ran the sheep off the ramps and onto the tightly-packed gravel. Spotty Dotty's crew were in the orchard and moving down to meet the newcomers, though, at a glance, I couldn't see one of the two black Spotty Dotty daughters which I used as marker ewes. I made a mental note to look out for her when I set up the mineral feeders.

I'd have to be quick, though. There was still plenty of water in the channel, but there wouldn't be for long. About twenty minutes leeway was all I had at best.

The granulated salt and minerals are heavy, the plastic feeders awkward, but I had them off the boat and deposited above the tide line in jig time. It was when I carried the feeders up to the sheltered place behind the lilac hedge that I saw Spotty Dotty's missing daughter. She was lying down, apparently unable to get up. As I moved closer I saw that she appeared to have caught her foot in something which held her fast. Whatever it was was obscured by tamped-down brush - last year's blackberry runners, raspberry canes and hardhack - which had been bent by the heavy weight of last winter's snow.

I knelt beside the black ewe and pushed the brush away. Her leg was caught in a metal ring. I pulled at the ring, but it was firmly anchored, and, as I yanked away more of the clinging runners and broken canes, I could see that it was firmly attached to boards which were weathered but not rotted. Odd again, I thought, but was too intent on freeing the ewe and getting off the island before the channel emptied to do anything more than file this new oddity at the back of my mind with the others.

I moved the black ewe's foot around in the ring and persuaded her to stand up, praying that the leg hadn't been broken. I was thankful that she was tame enough to let me help her. Slowly, I eased her hoof out of the metal circle. She stood up and walked off stiffly, limping a little - not her usual spry self, but not a casualty either.

I ran back to the beach for the salt and mineral mix, lugged the bags up to the feeders, filled them and raced back to the boat, Jen and Inkerman running in circles around me, enthusiastic participants in what they assumed was a new game. The three of us jumped aboard and put out just in the nick of time.

-7-

Jim was at my house - which is really his house - when I returned from the island. He hasn't lived in it since his marriage broke up about four years ago. Now, when he returns to the Bay, he stays with Vernon and Martha. I was especially pleased to see him, even though all through dinner he poked fun at my account of my day's 'sightings'. He'd listened to the tale of my outing without interrupting ... and then he'd laughed - long and loud.

But thanks to Jim's ribbing I'd picked up on one thing that seemed important to me and made my findings seem more real and more intriguing as well - though I didn't say so just then. When he'd identified the spot where I'd found the black ewe as the site of his grandfather's root cellar, he said that the ring couldn't possibly be held fast in the wood. The boards, he asserted, had to have rotted. No one, he assured me, would have replaced them in the last forty-odd years.

I was going to bring up the Belvederes, but by then Jim had turned his guns on my 'imaginary' Zodiac. Teasing me about this mystery craft took all his attention, and he hadn't found my story hard to shoot holes in.

"A Zodiac!" he joked as he poured out the wine he'd bought to go with the reheated lasagna. "A Zodiac, shooting out of a cave on the receding tide! Honestly, Angela, what would we do without your imagination to liven things up!

"I can't imagine, though, how even you came up with that one. It's so far-fetched. No one around here owns a Zodiac. And, by the way, are you sure you'd recognize one if you saw it? I bet you saw a log - part of a boom even - swept out on the last of the tide. When we were kids and Dad took us out there we used to watch for stuff that the caves - especially that last one - would spit out. Everything that came out was broken - even logs - after being beaten against those rock walls all those hours. Nothing - and no one - could survive that sort of thrashing. And of course when the cave's full of water a person would drown - apart from being beaten to a pulp."

Jim was turning pedantic now, lecturing me, explaining in detail the way he does to his computer customers. When he does that it drives me crazy, but it's no more use trying to shut him up once he's started on a tack like this than it is trying to turn the tide early.

"No one around here owns a Zodiac," Jim repeated, thinking, I suppose, that I hadn't heard him the first time. "Maybe in midsummer a visiting yachtsman - a really rich one - cruising the Bay might be pulling one in place of a dingy: the way midsummer tourists who take to the road in the fancier mobile homes often have a car fastened on behind to use when they're stopped for the night. But yachtsmen never turn up around here at this time of year. If they can afford a natty sailboat and are trailing a Zodiac, they're probably going to be down in the Caribbean."

This wasn't fun any more. It was turning into a harangue. Jim wasn't laughing, and I was regretting having told him what I'd seen. I suddenly felt weary.

"I'm tired," I said. "I'm going to bed. I don't want to talk any more." Though in truth I hadn't been able to get a word in edgeways since I'd told my story.

Jim knows I don't like his extended lectures, and he was suddenly apologetic - though he didn't say so. I could see him searching his mind for something which would right the mood. Promptly he found it.

"Tell you what," he said, once again the cheery self I'm so charmed by, "I'm free tomorrow. Suppose we go over to the island then and dump off another load of the critters. We'll come right back, and then I'll take you to town for dinner - and a movie, if there's anything on worth seeing. I bet Baxter would like to come along too. By tomorrow night it's going to be bad on the water, but that won't interfere with us driving to town."

-8-

Our trip to the island the next day was uneventful. "Not too many Zodiacs out and about!" Jim announced with mock seriousness as he pretended to scan the shoreline in search of some rare trespasser, all the while grinning like the troublesome ten-year-old he'd been when my brothers and I first spent half our summer holidays at Vernon and Martha's.

We got the sheep ashore and were home before the bad weather set in. It arrived on cue, just as Jim had predicted. No sooner had we stepped into the kitchen and closed the back door than the rising wind began to drive freezing rain against the big windows overlooking the garden and the sea. In short order each small pane was glazed with ice. The room darkened. Only the smudged outlines of the spruces bordering the garden could be seen. Going to town on such a night was out of the question. The road would be like a skating rink. Jim said that, if he waited much longer, he'd have trouble getting as far as his parents' house, even with the four wheel drive. Serious now - no longer the teasing, smart aleck cousin - he pulled up the hood of his parka and went out into the driving sleet. He had trouble shutting the storm door.

By the next morning half a foot of snow covered the ground. By noon it had melted, only to be replaced the following night. Day after day like this went by until I thought we'd never see the sun again.

As I brought my ledger up to date and wrote letters at the big kitchen table by the window, I kept glancing out to sea, hoping for a break in the weather. Nothing except fog or driving rain and snow was visible.

*   *   *

As the days passed without much letup, Vernon and Martha dropped by when they could to cheer me up. Vernon had to keep reminding me that weather like this was normal for what passes as spring in these parts. I know that's true, but every spring I hope that the leaves and flowers will come out early, that the sun will be warm as the T.V. weatherman indicates it is elsewhere. I couldn't help fretting about the sheep on the island.

"Don't you worry now, my dear," Vernon would say, "sheep have survived weather like this hereabouts for hundreds of years. They've good warm coats and enough to eat. If need be, they'll paw through the snow and ice, and if what they find underneath doesn't suit them, they'll march down to the beach and graze on seaweed. Lots of goodness in that.

"Besides, the ewes I kept, and my people before me, weren't such hardy girls as yours. I thought I had fine ones, but, though I hate to admit it, yours are better. Those Romanov fullbloods and crosses are tough. Not the prettiest sheep in the world, I'd say, but among the toughest. I almost think they like a taste of snow. Reminds them, maybe, of their ancestors' survival in the old days in Mother Russia."

I'm surprised Vernon has such a high opinion of my Romanovs. Not that they're not every bit as good as he says, but most people around here wouldn't admit it. Despite his age, Vernon's views are not as dyed-in-the-wool as most of our neighbors'. He's surprisingly open to change.

I like the way he tends to look optimistically towards the future - both about the sheep and the weather. He keeps telling me that he's sure my breeding stock will be in big demand before long - that I'll have a waiting list when it really sinks into the provincial mind here how prolific and hardy my sheep are. He's kept reminding me too that the sun should be out in full force before long, that we'll have lots of weather like the day I took the first load of sheep to the island - only better.

"There's many more of those fine days in the offing," he'll say, puffing calmly on the pipe which is forever clamped between his teeth. "And mind now, all this wind and rain - the wet snow too - will bring out the leaves. Remember, Angela child" - and the way he said it, softly, I didn't even mind him calling me 'child' - "though we may have the worst springs in the world, we have the best summers and autumns."

-9-

Vernon was right as usual. When the weather finally cleared, the sun seemed stronger and warmer than on the day I'd taken the first load of sheep to the island. Nature had made marked and surprising advances towards summer despite almost two weeks of snow and sleet. The grass in the front yard was green, and, in the lee of the house, the elderberry bush had leafed out.

I was all set to take the final contingent of sheep to the island. The tides were ideal and Jen and Inkerman seemed as enthusiastic as I was to get going. When I'd packed a considerable lunch for what promised to be a full day's outing, we set off.

Although Jim had promised to come along and give me a hand, he'd had to back out at the last moment. A client had called from Saint John, and, after he'd cleared up whatever problem he found there, he had to fly to Boston for a meeting. I was on my own again.

Perhaps because of that last trip over with Jim, when everything seemed so normal, or maybe because of all the time that had elapsed, I no longer felt apprehensive. The cigarettes, even the Zodiac, must have reasonable explanations, I told myself. In fact, I was beginning to agree with Jim, that what had looked to me like a Zodiac, must not have been. Perhaps, what I'd seen was indeed just an oddly-shaped log, the 'man', a limb - though I wasn't about to admit this to him.

Life, I recollected, is full of illusions. What about the time I'd seen what I thought was a spike on the road and had swerved to avoid it, landing up in the ditch? The policeman had shown me the small branch I'd been so sure was a spike. Doubtless Jim still remembered that accident and all the repairs the car had needed. It was nice of him not to dredge it up again, as lots of people would have. His teasing about the Zodiac had been irritating, but not meant to hurt.

It was hard to believe that anything could be amiss on such a perfect day as this. The Bay was smooth as silk and gleamed like polished silver, reflecting the black ducks boating on the surface, and, when I cut the motor just outside the cove, the air was so still that I could hear the beating of a seagull's wings as it circled the boat. A porpoise surfaced nearby and looked up at me, humorously I thought, and then lay basking companionably alongside.

Entranced, I recollected what Vernon had told me about these creatures. He'd described how, when he was a small boy and had gone fishing with his father in a rowboat, porpoises regularly came within a few inches of the gunwales. On one of these occasions his father had told how, in his own childhood, he'd watched the Indians shoot porpoises out here. In those days, he'd said, porpoise oil was burned in Fundy lighthouses and the Malecites and Micmacs on either side of the Bay had made a meager living killing these beautiful and intelligent mammals. Apparently the porpoises knew when they were being hunted and made themselves scarce so that only the Indians were consistently successful in shooting them and hauling in their carcasses before they sank from view and were lost.

Sad to imagine such friendly creatures being hunted, I thought as I looked down at *my* porpoise and smiled, pleased that in our times such slaughter was no longer necessary. And then it was time to start up the motor again. I moved into the channel, lulled by the peacefulness of everything around me. Even Jen and the sheep seemed more tranquil today. Getting them ashore had never seemed easier.

-10-

In this mood I began my tour of the island. I found the sheep I'd taken over on previous occasions congregated near the runoff from the spring where the grass was now lush and dark green. Spotty Dotty, her two black daughters and all the rest were there, hale and hearty.

"Vernon was right," I said aloud to Inkerman and Jen. "They're none the worse for having been out in all the bad weather." Inkerman wagged his tail, agreeable as usual.

Unlike the last time I'd been here, I felt no uneasiness - no sense of being watched. Perhaps, I thought, that was because I now had Inkerman with me. I knew he'd bristle if anyone were lurking.

I watched him charge into the stream which ran from the spring. He wallowed in the icy water, clearly delighted.

Jen moved quickly and purposefully up to the spring and began to drink delicately from near the source. She was not about to get wet unnecessarily. I followed her, looking forward to having a drink myself and to splashing the frigid water on my face. In this sheltered place it was surprisingly warm. I took off my jacket and knelt down on the large flat rock beside the spring.

It was then that I saw the deep imprint of a large boot in the moss beside the cask. It was longer and wider - much deeper too - than any footprint I might make and as distinguishable from ordinary bootprints by the deep indentations on the sole as tractor treads are from car treads.

The print was recent, all the indentations still clearly defined. How recent I couldn't say: I'm no expert scrutinizer of footprints. But I surmised that, if it had been exposed for even a few days to the driving rain and snow we'd had, the outlines would have begun to blur.

It couldn't have been today's though, what with no boat but mine in the cove and no building to hide - or shelter - anyone. And again I was back to the question I'd asked myself before, the question that Jim and Vernon had asked as well: Why would anyone else but us want to be here at this time of year?

I gave up pondering. No point trying on my own to figure out all these odd signs that no one else had seen and no one else believed in. I'd have to get Jim or Vernon, or both of them, to come back with me on some pretext - and, soon, before the footprint vanished.

If I couldn't clear up these mysteries I wasn't going to be able to carry on. Increasingly I was frightened to be here alone, and if this fear persisted I'd have to get rid of the sheep and consequently change my life. I wasn't prepared to do that. I liked things the way they were. Besides, pasturing so many sheep on the mainland was simply not feasible. The family doesn't have enough land there, and fencing what we do have is too costly a proposition just now. Sheep need such strong fences to keep them in and roving dogs and coyotes out. The island is so perfect as a sheep pasture, I reflected for the umpteenth time. If only I could figure out what was happening here!

I sat looking at the sheep so peacefully grazing in this idyllic situation, and felt ready to weep with frustration. Everything was perfect except for the unexplained signs of an intruder's presence. Even Spotty Dotty and her progeny were on their best behavior. Idly I watched her adventurous daughters, my black marker sheep, grazing tranquilly at the front of the flock.

And then my mind reverted to the scene I'd witnessed on my earlier visit to the island when the black sheep had been caught in the ring. I replayed the whole brief scene in my mind. It came back vividly. What about that ring, so firmly attached to the weathered boards? And why hadn't those boards rotted? Peculiar! No doubt about it!

The only way to satisfy myself, and, I hoped, set my mind at rest permanently, was to go and look at the old root cellar while I was alone on the island. If the deeply-dug hole had kept vegetables and apples frost-free and dry in the old days, it might, I reasoned, now contain produce equally valuable to contemporary residents of these parts.

Jim had instantly remembered its existence when I'd mentioned the ring in which Spotty Dotty's daughter had been caught. Considering the close connection between people in these parts - relationships going back to childhood and to earlier generations as well - it was more than likely that others would remember about this root cellar too. Maybe someone Jim's age. He'd often told me that, when he was a child and Vernon had ferried the sheep over to the island, he'd been allowed to take along at least one playmate. The boys had roamed the island between tides.

-11-

The blackberry bushes, which had prospered and proliferated in the vicinity of the root cellar, almost hid the door. These brambles had spread out and matted. Some had latched onto the boards so firmly that no sensible person would think of venturing into this thorny jungle.

If it hadn't been for Spotty Dotty's adventurous daughter, I'd certainly never have considered picking my way through the thorny tangle. I hadn't minded the thorns so much the day I'd rescued her: I'd had my work gloves on then, but this time I'd left them on the boat and I really felt the barbs. I was getting a sort of high-powered multi-needle treatment - free acupuncture - I told myself, trying to make light of the situation.

But moving among the blackberry bushes was a lot more painful than acupuncture and without any benefits that I could imagine. The pricks increased my level of stress. The more I concentrated on yanking the brambles aside, the deeper their barbs penetrated my hands and wrists, drawing blood. I wished again for a good pair of protective work gloves.

But at length I had the door exposed in its entirety. The weathered boards, probably from a barn, appeared to be nailed to something more substantial beneath. When I grasped the ring so that I could see what indeed was below, I noticed that the screws used to attach it to the boards were old, rusted. And the nails in the boards - square-headed ones, unavailable these days - were also rusty.

Suddenly my suspicions seemed foolish. I'd read too many Nancy Drew mysteries when I was growing up, I thought. I was glad that neither Jim nor Vernon was here to mock me. It was, I thought, certainly not worth going to so much trouble to look down into an old root cellar. And if the door had been replaced sometime in the last fifteen years or so - well, so what? Any local fishermen who wanted to stash gear in the old cellar might reuse the old nails and screws when rebuilding the door. Most of the old-timers never wasted a thing. Probably whoever had repaired the door had wanted to store extra fuel for the motor. Or maybe nets and traps. Who knew? Who cared? None of my business.

Anyway, there I was, cut and torn from my struggle with the brambles, and I told myself that I might as well have a look. The door was flush with the ground and consequently heavy to lift. Only when I pulled back on the ring with all my strength was I able to fling it aside. There, backing the weathered boards, were more weathered boards, these nailed crossways. No wonder the door was so heavy!

This was not a slipshod job. Whoever had taken all this trouble had obviously had proper tools and considerable foresight. He had clearly intended that the root cellar should be usable for quite some time. But then, why not? Even gas and oil, tools and fishing gear needed to be stored in a safe place. They were all expensive enough to replace when you totalled them up. Not to mention the bother if you couldn't put your hands on them when you counted on their being handy.

Still, unaccountably, I was excited - too excited to be frightened. I smiled at the vague suspicions which had haunted me previously on the mainland. Seeming problems invariably are easier to cope with - some even evaporate - when you're face to face with them, when your're not troubled by idle imaginings.

I stared down at the old steps, leading into the space beneath. The root cellar seemed to be more than a hole in the ground. At the bottom of the steps - a good ten feet down - was what appeared to be a tunnel angling off horizontally towards the cliffs. The entrance was buttressed by hand-hewn posts, so that it looked more like the entryway to an old-fashioned, hand-dug mine shaft - the kind you see in pictures illustrating mining in the later phases of the California or Yukon gold rushes ... after placer mining was exhausted - than a root cellar.

I lay down, taking my flashlight out of my pocket and directing its beam towards this dark opening. Though it's so small, it casts a long bright light. I thought this way I might see whatever was immediately inside.

Just then Inkerman came bounding up, worried, I suppose, when I'd lain down and disappeared from his sight. His enthusiastic, welcoming bunt when he spotted me knocked my arm against the door frame. The flashlight sailed out of my hand and landed on the dirt at the bottom of the steps. I had to go down after it. Amazingly, the bulb hadn't broken. As the L.L. Bean catalog description had promised, the flashlight was "small but rugged."

I climbed down the steps, Inkerman at my heels, Jen pushing by me. Although Inkerman didn't like stairs, even, I supposed, an abbreviated set like these, he nevertheless descended them without complaint or persuasion, having presumably made the snap decision that accompanying me, whatever the circumstances, would be preferable to being left behind.

I was surprised that the steps, though appearing to be old, were not rickety. I looked around from my new vantage point. The earth in the root cellar seemed undisturbed. Fleetingly, I wished Vernon and Jim were here. They would remember what it had been like. They would KNOW whether any of the part I could see had been touched since they'd last seen it.

Without my pocket flashlight I wouldn't have been able to venture beyond the entrance. It was a stroke of luck that I'd brought it along - for my proposed foray into the fourth cave, not for this. Standing at the entrance, I shone the light inside - expecting some unusual revelation - finding, instead ... nothing. Just an ordinary root cellar, the shelves on both sides sagging with the decrepitude of age, an old barrel and a dozen or so dust-laden jars set to one side and long since abandoned. No repair work here. No faked oldness. Everything WAS old.

Taking another step forward, I was suddenly on rock, not just paving stones which had been carried there, but solid rock. I made a mental note that the cliff rock must extend further inland than one might have expected. The light showed that the walls, and ceiling too, had now graduated into rock, the ancient marks of a hand tool, perhaps a chisel, apparent throughout. I marvelled that anyone should have gone to so much trouble, and in so remote a place. So long ago! For there was no sign on the rocks of recent work. Small wonder that Vernon and Jim had remembered the existence of this root cellar! It was extraordinary.

As I stood marvelling and wondering I shone the light into the back of the cellar, some eight or nine feet away from where I stood. More shelves... The wood old... These were, however, made of rough lumber, not planed like the wood of which the adjoining shelves had been made. They did not sag as much as those along the sides either. Instead, they appeared to be firmly attached. And my light revealed that the wall behind these shelves was also of rough boards, not rock, as I would have expected. I guessed that they had been built by the same careful carpenter who had repaired the trap door.

But for what purpose? The new shelves were empty. Moreover, there wasn't room enough on them to hold a large quantity of anything - only enough for the fifty or so jars of pickles and jams I made every fall, mostly for presents. It almost looked as if they were a front for something else, or, like a theatre prop, briefly convincing enough to con a casual observer into believing that they were just abandoned shelves in an old root cellar. Or was this thought, I wondered, just my active imagination at work again?

Once more Inkerman bumped me - a typical 'Labraboor,' Jim would have said. He'd found something too which interested him. He whined softly, demanding that I pay attention to whatever it was.

He was focused intently on something under the bottom shelf. It was impossible to see what from where I stood. But it was apparent that he had something between his teeth. He tugged. Nothing happened. Whatever he was yanking on was attached.

"Drop it, Inkerman. Drop it," I insisted. And it was only when Inkerman reluctantly let go and stepped back that the entire rear wall swung back. As it swung, I could see a looped rope attached to the weathered boards behind the lowest shelf. That was what Inkerman had had his teeth fixed in. Inkerman had always had a fixation on ropes. My mind flashed back over all the times, from puppyhood, when he had preferred retrieving them to anything else and had dragged them back from the beach.

The rope reminded me at once of the other rope I'd seen on the island. As far as I could remember, this was about the same thickness and color as the piece I'd seen dangling from the roof of the fourth cave.

What I saw before me - essentially a furnished room - was totally unexpected. Yet I felt surprisingly self-possessed. Here was evidence of something unusual - firm evidence indeed. Wouldn't Jim - and Vernon too - have to eat crow? I thought. Or would they? Was it possible that they knew? A nagging doubt.

I could scarcely contain my excitement. I was on the verge, I felt sure, of a momentous discovery. I was alone on the island, still with several free hours before the tide was right for my getaway. No one else could bring a boat in until the tide returned. I was convinced that it was safe for me to explore this room at my leisure.

-12-

I found myself standing at the top of eight or nine wide steps chiseled from the rock face and leading down into what appeared to be a huge natural cave. The cave was not dark and dank like the root cellar, but dimly lit and ventilated by a considerable number of irregularly-shaped slots and holes high up on one side of the vaulted ceiling. One of these openings was quite large, probably about two feet by three, and, although all the openings appeared to be natural, the largest, because it could let in the rain, had been fitted meticulously with a glass panel. This panel could, apparently, be opened or closed by manipulating a metal rod which extended from the side of this skylight to about five feet from the floor of the cave.

The skylight was open. I could hear the gulls calling near it and see them soaring back and forth. Some of the smaller openings were inhabited by birds I judged to be cliff swallows.

Cliff ... swallows. Cliffs... These openings, I surmised then, had to be high in the side of the cliffs above Shag Islet and over the four caves visible from the sea and approachable from the beach at low tide. That meant that the cave I surveyed was pretty much directly above these beach caves - far enough above, indeed, to be out of reach of the highest tides. And because this elevated cave seemed so airy I assumed that it was not joined to any of the caves beneath it which were washed by the sea.

I walked down the steps and surveyed my surroundings in amazement. Ordinarily I was leery of caves, but this one was very pleasant, fresh and almost homey. Whoever inhabited it had taken considerable trouble to make it comfortable and keep it neat. There were three camp cots with a sleeping bag folded on the end of each, a couple of kerosene heaters, a primus stove for cooking, a folding table and three chairs. On the table was an oil lamp. Several more were affixed to niches in the cave wall.

Off to one side were boxes - hundreds of boxes of various shapes and sizes, neatly stacked, and, behind them, cupboards recently built. The lumber was new and there had been no attempt made to disguise this newness. The cupboards must have been thirty feet long. As well, they extended from floor to ceiling so that a long step-ladder was required to reach the top doors.

Everything about this setup suggested permanence. Whatever project was underway here, it was clearly not intended to be a short-term one.

As my eyes grew more accustomed to the light, I could see that there appeared to be some sort of anteroom on the side underneath the apertures. I approached this darkness hesitantly, directing the beam of my flashlight onto the floor before me and feeling my way, so that I would not trip on the somewhat uneven floor or fall into a hole. Spraining an ankle, breaking a leg - or worse - would, I thought, have been particularly unfortunate in this situation.

All at once the rock floor petered out into a plywood slab - apparently a movable platform. I stopped, raised the light a little and saw, resting on the plywood platform, a Zodiac. A Zodiac with a jet motor attached to the stern.

So I hadn't been mistaken!

Buffering the platform on all sides was chunky tubing, of automobile inner tube diameter and apparently air-filled. I guessed that when the platform was let down into the lower cave some of the air must be released. Then when it was elevated again the tubing would be reinflated, making a snug, virtually draftless fit.

I shone the light back and forth around the boat and saw that it was unattached, though the platform had been elaborately secured by ropes looped through heavy metal rings embedded in the rock. These ropes appeared to be roughly the same weight and color as the others, and like them were new. The metal rings, however, were obviously old. Rust had rubbed off them onto the ropes.

Suddenly I felt panicky. What if the owner of the Zodiac was already on the island and about to return to the cave any moment? Or what if whoever it was who'd invested so much time and money in this undertaking returned on the next tide in a larger boat? There must be a larger boat involved, I reasoned. You couldn't very well bring all this stuff in in an open boat like the Zodiac.

"We'd better get out of here before we get any older," I told Inkerman anxiously. "And be all set to push off as soon as we can."

And then I began to realize what a truly narrow escape I'd had already. Supposing a person or persons had come in on the Zodiac shortly before I'd arrived, while there was water in the cave, but not enough to block it or make entering it particularly dangerous? He or they would have been in the cave when I'd found my way in. What might have happened then was anyone's guess. Certainly the possibilities were not agreeable to contemplate.

And to think I had gone about my business believing that no one could possibly be on the island because no boat was anchored in the channel! My mind, churning, again brought me sharply up against the terrifying thought that a dangerous stranger - maybe more than one - might be wandering the island at that very moment. If he was, he would surely return to the cave and discover me.

"Come on, boy," I said to Inkerman again. "Let's get out of here."

Inkerman wagged his tail and grinned, clearly delighted to be spoken to again. I looked around for Jen. I didn't want to have to come back for her. But she was nowhere to be seen. I supposed she'd stayed put. I did not remember her following me into the cave. I'd told her to lie down just after we climbed down into the root cellar, so I supposed she was still lying at the bottom of the steps, obediently awaiting my next command. Probably she had her eyes fixed firmly on the passageway, hoping perhaps that I'd emerge with some sheep for her to herd.

"One quick look into a box and a cupboard. Then we'll go," I explained, as much to myself as to Inkerman. "I HAVE to know."

Most of the boxes were piled too high for me to get at them easily. Besides, they had been taped, as if for shipping. Only one near the table had been opened, the tape cut. I pulled aside the flaps, and there inside were cartons of Belvederes. One had been opened.

So it was from this stash that the pack I'd found on the other side of the island must have come! Interesting! Most interesting! Smuggled cigarettes? They had to be.

And then I looked at the knife on the table - probably the knife that had slit open the box, I guessed. It looked familiar. I picked it up and turned it over. It was distinctive. The handle a mottled green and red, the blade razor sharp. It looked identical to the knife I'd given Jim for his last birthday. I'd had it made especially for him by a man who made knives by hand and sold them in the Saint John market.

My Irish grandmother, if she'd been alive and known about it, would have told me I should have known better. She'd always said you should NEVER give a knife as a present. It was the worst kind of bad luck. If you did, she'd said, the only way you could avoid disaster was to get the recipient to pay for the gift. "A penny will do," she'd said. "Just a token payment." I'd never exacted that token payment. Silly to be superstitious, I told myself.

Jim, I recalled, had lost the knife almost at once. Thought he'd left it behind at Baxter's, but, when he called, Baxter'd said he hadn't seen it since the night of the party. That had been almost a year earlier.

-13-

Jim's birthday party was at Baxter's again this year. Baxter had insisted. He liked to cook and Jim's birthday was, he said, his only opportunity in the course of an entire year to prepare a real spread. And what a lavish and luscious feast it was!

I've always thought that Baxter could have been head chef at the Hyatt Regency - or any other swish place. Whatever the occasion, he takes such elaborate pains to have everything perfect. Just getting together all the makings for a party like this must have occupied the best part of a week - and then the day before the do he'd have had to go up to the Saint John market for perishables and several special sauces and relishes he liked to buy from a stall there. As for the lobsters, he believed in buying them from the pound the very day they were to be cooked. Even then he wouldn't settle for just any lobster. Each one had to suit his specifications.

Whoever waited on Baxter needed a lot of patience. I knew from experience. I'd gone to the pound with him once and been exasperated and embarrassed about the time he took to make his purchase.

While Baxter had paid at the front desk, I'd stayed behind to apologize to the woman who'd pulled the valuable crustaceans out of the tank. She just smiled and said, "Oh well, that's Baxter. He'll try your patience some, but he's a good boy at heart - and never strong. Not sturdy like his dad. I feel sorry for him. Not being able to fish like everyone else. Lucky his folks left him well-fixed, so he doesn't have to work steady. Couldn't do it.

"His mum and I were friends right up to the time of the crash and she always worried about just keeping him alive, what with his asthma and allergies and all. Funny thing though, he seems stronger these days."

*   *   *

Baxter and Jim had been friends as far back as anyone could remember. Lyle and Mac had been the other two members of their gang. 'The frightful foursome,' Vernon still called them laughingly. As children he'd often taken them all out on his boat fishing, but told everyone that whenever he put them ashore they were always up to some sort of devilment - except for Baxter. But that was only because Baxter didn't feel well enough, he'd reckoned.

Baxter had tried to keep up with his stronger friends, Vernon had told me once, but he got sick a lot, missed school and had to stay home with his mother. "Smart lady, Baxter's mum!" Vernon had reminisced. "She taught that boy all sorts of things - how to cook and how to figure things out for himself. She was always carting books home from the library - books on everything. She didn't want him to miss out - him being the only one and all. And she seems to have done the right thing. Baxter never misses a trick. Anything you can't get a handle on - anything to do with figures or computers anyway - go see Baxter. That's what Jim does when he's stuck. I've never seen Baxter at a loss yet. He just figures away till be gets whatever it is."

*   *   *

I had arrived at the party early, along with Jim, Martha and Vernon. We thought we might be able to give Baxter a hand with any last moment chores. Apart from Baxter, who was fussing over the flower arrangement on the table, only the other two members of the 'frightful foursome' were there. Lyle and Mac promptly went into a huddle with Jim. Myrna, Lyle's wife, was away looking after her sick mother.

I didn't feel like talking. Hadn't felt like coming to the party. I wasn't in the right mood. My thoughts were still on the island. I felt frustrated because I hadn't had a chance to tell Jim or Vernon what had happened to me there earlier in the week. But there hadn't been time to fill them in. According to Martha, Jim had only arrived home in time to change for the party.

Baxter told me to help myself to the drinks and *hors d'oeuvres* set out on the sideboard. Smilingly, still retiring in manner though we'd known each other now ever since that first summer I'd stayed with Vernon and Martha when I was only twelve, he warned me that I'd better settle in for a considerable wait before supper. All the people who had come last year had been invited, he said, and he reminded me that couples like the Rawlins and the McGivners never got anywhere on time.

I was pleased to have this information. With everyone together again, I could study them, play the sleuth, try to figure out who might have picked up Jim's knife - if it was indeed Jim's knife - and taken it to the cave. Who could be the cigarette smuggler - or smugglers?

Perhaps it was just as well I hadn't had a chance to tell Jim what had happened. Jim was not notable for his discretion. He might have blurted the whole story out, wanting to entertain everyone. Then, if the smuggler - or smugglers - were present, they'd know we knew what they were up to. The mere thought of that happening made me feel shaky. I resolved to keep my discoveries to myself until I had something more to go on. A depressing resolve because I felt I needed help.

While I was filling my plate with the delicate tidbits Baxter had prepared, I was aware of someone brushing against my skirt. And there was Bruiser, Baxter's yellow lab and Inkerman's brother, looking up at me expectantly and wagging his tail.

Bruiser and I were always delighted to see one another. He'd been my puppy before he was Baxter's. Thisbe, his mother, and Inkerman's, had been my first lab. I'd even given Bruiser his name because, as a very young puppy, he'd been so sturdy and aggressive - the strongest of the litter and the most outgoing and advanced for his age. He was the first of the nine pups to figure everything out. A beautiful looking dog too. If Baxter hadn't wanted him so badly, I'd have kept him as well as Inkerman. Bruiser seemed aware of this special relationship and never failed to make a fuss over me. Tonight I was especially pleased. I knelt down to pat him and talk to him. And suddenly I felt happier. Perhaps the evening was going to be all right after all.

And as for my nagging worries about the island and what was going on there, I'd just have to wait and watch - carefully. Maybe the later part of this evening would yield a clue. Once everyone was together someone might make a false move, say or do something suspicious. Everyone who'd been here last year - anyone who might have picked up Jim's knife and taken it to the island, for instance - was, I thought, suspect.

I looked across the room at Jim talking with Lyle and Mac. What if the culprits were those three? Or one or two of them? If Jim knew, but wasn't involved, would he tell?

-14-

I followed Bruiser into the kitchen thinking that Baxter might need help, but he obviously had everything under control. Glasses, plates and cutlery were neatly laid out, and, ready to go into the oven, was what I judged to be the evening's *pièce de résistance*, even more significant than the lobsters, which were not in sight. A huge pastry salmon lay bridging two large cookie tins: scales, eyes, tail, all the contours were sculpted to perfection.

"It's marvellous," I gasped, overwhelmed by the sight of this masterpiece. "I've never seen anything like it." And then, curious about what the pastry hid, I blurted out, "What's inside the crust?"

Baxter smiled diffidently, though not I judged with displeasure. Despite his many talents, he often seemed to lack self-confidence in social situations... perhaps partly the result of his prolonged bouts of ill health, particularly in childhood. My unqualified admiration obviously pleased him.

"Just a concoction of mine - a *pâté* with salmon and herbs. The stuffed pastry fish should look more authentic when it comes out of the oven, provided, of course, the innards don't run and I cook it lightly," he noted, surveying his handiwork critically, then adding, "I'm hoping the tandoori I've rubbed on - sparingly - will provide just the right rosy tinge when it's done." He pointed to a reddish powder on the still pale pastry.

Baxter, the precision expert, and Baxter, the artist, had merged in this production. I was impressed and intimidated.

Dreaming up such a culinary work of art is beyond me, and, even if it were within my capabilities, I'd never be able to bring myself to make the effort. I couldn't even imagine how long it had taken him. It always seems to me that my own plain - very plain - cooking takes too much of the day. The leg of lamb I'd cooked earlier and brought over in the roasting pan as a contribution to the feast is about as complicated as my cooking gets.

Baxter's putting on this spread had spared Vernon, Martha and me the trouble of trying to have Jim's birthday party at their house or mine - exempted Martha and me from the elaborate preparations I'd have found so frustrating and Martha is not really up to any more. I felt deeply grateful. Something else I owed Baxter. He is the kindest and most unassuming person I know. Jim's best friend and mine. Always doing things for other people when he sees they can't cope themselves. Never expecting, it would seem, anything in return.

Bruiser had stretched out on the floor between the counter and the stove, absolutely attentive now to his master's labors. His eyes followed Baxter's every move appreciatively. He didn't, however, need to ask what the pastry hid. His Labrador nose identified its essences.

I'd like to have stayed in the kitchen to watch Baxter at work. Bruiser had the best spot in the house I thought. I wanted to tell Baxter what an astounding success he'd be on a T.V. cooking show, but I refrained. I sensed that he didn't really like having me in the kitchen, that, good friends as we were, my questions - even my compliments - spoiled his concentration on the last minute details.

I understood how he felt. Even when I'm preparing a simple

family meal with Vernon, Martha and Jim as guests, I get addled when one of them comes into the kitchen to talk to me. I forget to serve the rolls or make the gravy in time. Some such thing.

I wandered back into the living room, taking a sip of my drink as I surveyed the scene. Most of the guests had arrived during my brief sojourn in the kitchen. Lyle and Mac were the welcoming committee, a duty they appeared to take seriously. They were getting drinks for those who were reluctant to pour their own and were passing the *hors d'oeuvres*.

In the spacious living room, which had, Baxter told me, once been two sitting rooms connected by French doors - now replaced by a wide archway - there was no crowding. A few people were still chatting in the entrance hall, a space larger than my living room. But most had congregated in the dining room, within reach of the drinks and *hors d'oeuvres*.

The big house seemed particularly welcoming and festive that night, its old-fashioned charm and elegance without ostentation. It had been built by Baxter's great-grandfather, a sea captain, in the days when native woods were available cheaply and close at hand - a time when families were expected to run to ten or twelve children and visiting, even resident, relatives were commonplace and accepted.

The baseboards and some of the paneling are butternut. Because of this wood's soft natural lustre, it needs no varnish or polish. Vernon told me once when I'd remarked on how much I loved the butternut used in this house that *the old man* - his usual appellation for Baxter's great-grandfather, despite the fact that the burly captain never reached old age and had lived out his life long before Vernon was born - had loved this wood too.

"No problem coming by butternut then," Vernon had said. "I've heard tell, there was a big stand of them up back on the ridge. All gone now in these parts. The Indians used to extract a kind of butter from the nuts. That's supposed to be how the trees got their name."

Fires had been lit in both fireplaces in the main room and in the franklin in the dining room. The warm and steady glow from the birch and maple logs made these *public rooms*, as the old-timers called their more formal rooms for entertaining, especially welcoming during this still chilly spring evening. I wondered idly whether Baxter had also made up the fire in his study, but I guessed not. I'd noticed when we arrived that the door from the hall into that special sanctuary was shut. I supposed Baxter didn't want anyone careless wandering in and perhaps spilling a drink on some of the valuable reference books he tended to leave open there - or tinkering with his computer and inadvertently deleting an important entry. Baxter is careful with his most prized possessions. Well, actually, Baxter is meticulous about everything.

The other study door, which opens from the dining room, was also shut and the Boston rocker, which usually sits beside the franklin, had been placed in front of this door, likely to discourage anyone from idly turning the handle and discovering this room. If I hadn't known better, I'd have supposed that this door led into a closet. That was doubtless what Baxter had intended a casual visitor to think - not that most of his invited guests could be termed casual visitors.

Moving the rocker had exposed more of the large oval braided rug on which it usually sat. Baxter's great-grandmother, the sea captain's wife, had made it. I supposed she'd spent evening after evening sitting by this franklin, or one like it, braiding and stitching while her husband had been at sea - times when the children had been put to bed. In those days of candles and coal oil lamps children went to bed early. And if ever a house had been made for children, this was it, I thought tonight, as I often had. Sad that Baxter likely wouldn't have any, that he was probably the end of his family's line. The sea captain and his wife had had four children before his ship foundered off Briar Island one wild November night. Two of these had died of childhood illnesses. The remaining daughter had been a spinster. Only Baxter's grandfather had married. He had had just one child, Baxter's father. Baxter, in turn, was an only child. As far as I knew Baxter had shown no inclination to marry. The house, it seemed, would one day pass to strangers.

The deep window seats beneath the bay windows had lids which lifted up to reveal deep storage boxes. There were still toys at the bottom of one of these. Baxter had shown them to me years ago when he had given me a tour of the house. We were both teenagers then. The toys were ancient and battered, mostly wooden boats and a few animals. The paint which had once covered them had nearly worn off.

Not only toy boats had proliferated here. All the pictures in the house, apart from family portraits, were of nautical scenes. As well, on each broad mantel was a model sailing ship. The most elaborate and distinctive of these was displayed in what had been the front parlor. Her name, the *Angelina*, was clearly inscribed in cream - once white, I guessed - on the black hull. The sails, now faded, were pale slate blue, the mast was pine, and the diminutive cabin - what one could see of it - was paneled in butternut.

Still feeling somewhat anti-social, I walked over to have another look at the *Angelina*. The vessel had been reproduced in such detail that it merited close scrutiny. But what caught my attention at once, distracting me from the miniature sailing ship, were six packs of Belvederes stacked alongside the model. I couldn't help wondering where they'd come from. Baxter didn't smoke, couldn't smoke because of his asthma. Who had placed them there? I wondered. I looked around the room to see who was smoking.... Almost half the people in the room. I wondered what brand. Ridiculous to suspect these people. Most of them were friends.

I recalled what Vernon had said when I'd shown him the pack I'd found by the island spring: "Probably half the folks around here smoke that brand. Even if some of them get the odd few packs over the border more cheaply than here, so what? It's always been like that. Booze, smokes, whatever.... Pick them up when and where you can. S'long as no one gets hurt. This pipe tobacco, for instance, was a present. I didn't ask a lot of questions about where it came from...."

Still, I reminded myself, what I'd seen in the island cave didn't indicate the smuggling of the odd pouch, or even tin, of pipe tobacco, or a few packs of cigarettes. It had to be a large-scale operation if the contents of all those taped up boxes were the same as the one that had stood open.

-15-

Predictably, Chester and Howard and their wives were the last to arrive, and as usual their entry was a noisy one. The twins, Meg and Marie, made sure of that. They shrieked in response to Mac's welcoming bear hug and then went off upstairs arm in arm, laughing and chattering, to leave their coats on the bed in the large front bedroom.

Chester and Howard had married the O'Donnell twins four years earlier in a double ceremony, and since then, because their wives were inseparable, they had been obliged to spend a lot of time together. Unfortunately, Chester and Howard had much less in common than their wives. Chester fished while Howard sold insurance and real estate. Chester was quiet and self-contained, Howard loud and expansive.

In his penetrating voice Howard explained why they were late. "It's all Ches's fault," he bellowed. "Eh, Ches?" he said, laughing and clapping his brother-in-law on the shoulder so enthusiastically that, from where I stood, Chester appeared to wince under the blow. Whether Chester's response was physical or psychological - or both

- I could only guess. "Tell 'em about it, Boy," Howard roared.

When Chester said nothing, Howard carried on, obviously expecting to have his say anyway. He pushed into the living room interrupting all the conversations.

"Just kidding, folks," Howard boomed when he saw he had everyone's attention. "Not Chester's fault.... Damn tide.... Couldn't get the girls out of the store when Chester said it was time to go. Hell bent on picking out all their dooty frees.... Should've been back yesterday, and here we are now ... just off the boat. 'Fraid we'd miss out on this do altogether.... Can't get another feed like Baxter's anywhere else for love or money.... Hey, don't you agree with me?" he said to the room in general - pivoting in the center of the room to make sure his remarks had reached everyone, and clearly once more not expecting an answer.

"I see Howard's been into the sauce again," Vernon observed quietly at my elbow.

I'd been so intent on watching the new arrivals and so sure that no one had yet noticed my presence in the dark nook by the fireplace, that Vernon's voice made me jump. Jim was with his father and seemed about to say something when Howard came bearing down on us.

"Speaking of dooty frees," he announced, "here's some for the birthday boy." He laughed uproariously at a joke only he seemed to appreciate and thrust a package into Jim's hands. "No time for fancy wrapping. Sorry about that.... But happy birthday, Boy," he shouted, louder than before, clapping Jim on the back even more enthusiastically than he had Chester in the entrance hall.

Jim, momentarily off balance, collected himself and grinned, his usual good-humored self. No wonder, I thought, that Chester had seemed to wince. Blows like Howard's were enough to fell the proverbial ox.

"Got to make up for lost time now.... See you later." Howard moved off toward the sideboard.

Jim looked down into the brown paper bag Howard had thrust

into his hands, then, without speaking, passed the bag to Vernon and me. Inside were four cartons of Belvederes and a 40 ounce bottle of dark rum. Legal duty frees, if the four of them had indeed been across the border long enough. Also available at local stores - though, if they had been purchased locally, a quick calculation of their cost made them seem too expensive a present from a relatively casual acquaintance. I couldn't help wondering. What I'd seen in the cave made me suspicious of everyone.

Jim looked pleased, but surprised. After a quick glance, Vernon seemed to forget about the present. He appeared restless and inattentive. I realized that he was looking forward to having his supper and an early night. He turned to me and remarked in an undertone, "I'm too old for night life. Martha holds up better at a party than I do. Always did. I like my supper sitting down at a table - at five o'clock, or thereabouts. None of this standing 'round, holding drinks and making small talk till 'way after seven or eight, then sitting down in an armchair with a plate balanced on one knee."

As if he'd heard Vernon's complaint, Baxter came through the swinging door from the kitchen holding the largest platter I'd ever seen. On it was the pastry salmon, just out of the oven, lightly baked, the tandoori giving the skin a slight reddish tint and the entire concoction an exotic aroma.

Conversations stopped while everyone, awestruck by this centerpiece, gathered around the table. Harley Donald reached for his camcorder and the twins squealed as they rushed for the stairs to retrieve the polaroids they'd left in their purses in the upstairs bedroom. After presenting Jim with the knife and lifter and instructing him to cut into the pastry, Baxter returned to the kitchen.

And so the feast began. We were all drawn together over it, and, for a while, I suspended my scrutiny. Jim persuaded me to join him, Lyle and Mac. And after seating Vernon and Martha at a card table near the fire, Baxter pulled up a chair and sat down quietly between Jim and me. I think he must have been too tired to talk. But that was fine. Baxter, Jim and I didn't need to jabber away to feel comfortable with one another. Lyle and Mac, though the latter was not usually loquacious, did most of the talking, their observations uncontentious and often comic. Under the spell of feast and firelight, the five of us basked in a contentment none of us wanted disrupted.

-16-

The day after Baxter's party Jim and I made a quick trip to the island. Many times that day I was on the verge of telling Jim what I had discovered there. Yet each time I stopped myself, not because I didn't trust him, but because I feared for him if he knew what I knew. He is too open with everyone, too trusting. If he had learned then about the cave and its contents, he would, I thought, likely mention it to someone. The confidant he chose could well be the wrong person. Whoever was masterminding the island venture must have a local connection because he knew so much about the island. It was also clear that he had to be playing for high stakes since he had already made a considerable investment. Just how large this was I couldn't guess, though I knew that even the Zodiac was a costly purchase.

I made up my mind to bide my time, and then perhaps confide in Baxter. I felt sure that he would know the right thing to do. Thoughtful, wise and quietly competent, Baxter had lived so much to himself - was such a private person - that he wouldn't feel compelled to jump to conclusions or to share his knowledge and thoughts with the first passerby.

Vernon was another person with a mentality somewhat similar to Baxter's. But I was sure he would discuss whatever he was told with Martha, who might in turn tell Jim. She was almost sure to tell her sister, who would then probably confide in her husband, who...

Anyway, Vernon had come to the stage in his life when I suspected this information would be a burden he would rather not shoulder. For Baxter, on the other hand, getting to the bottom of whatever was happening on the island would, I imagined, be something of a game, a puzzle he'd enjoy figuring out.

*   *   *

The following morning I decided to drop in on Baxter, sound him out perhaps if the circumstances seemed propitious. I wasn't sure what I would say, but I thought I'd at least get him talking about the island trips Vernon had taken the boys on when they were young. I hoped he had noticed something then.

When I rang, no one answered. Both back and front doors were locked, but I guessed Baxter couldn't have gone far: the upstairs windows were open, the curtains moving gently in the breeze.

I walked down the path through the woods to the water - Baxter's favorite walk, he'd always said. Small wonder! White pines towered above me, the few token giants left from bygone days. And when I came out into a clearing colonized recently by young birches and maples, I stopped to pick a bouquet of the mayflowers which bordered the path.

Once in sight of the bay I noticed that the boathouse doors were open. "Baxter," I called out. "Hi! You in there?"

When I stepped inside I was close to the keel of Baxter's sailboat. It towered above me. From inside there were muffled scurrying sounds like a mouse in a box, but no reply. He hadn't heard me.

I'd never seen Baxter's boat out of the water before. It looked much larger in the boathouse than when it was moored among the fishing boats. As I stood looking up at the hull and wondering how to attract Baxter's attention, I realized that I had never looked closely at Baxter's boat before, never really thought about it either. He hadn't used it much: he hadn't been well enough. So I assumed he had kept it in mothballs most of the time. On the rare occasions when Baxter had mentioned sailing, he had spoken of being a fair weather sailor. He had offered to take me out, but something - the weather, illness or an appointment - always seemed to intervene. Besides, the season is so short here - especially for fair weather sailors.

Now it suddenly occurred to me that this yacht meant more to Baxter than anyone knew - not so much perhaps, I guessed, for the rare trips he actually took on her, but for the fantasy voyages she provided him with. Aesthetically too, she was an absorbing interest. Her sleek lines were beautiful, and just looking at her took one back in time. She was not a modern fiberglass model, but built of wood, a full-sized replica of the miniature *Angelina*. Baxter had told me once that the only man he could find who could build just the vessel he wanted lived near Lunenburg and came from a long line of shipbuilders. And as I stood looking up at the recently-painted black hull I surmised that the maintenance Baxter himself did on this boat was more like a curator's upkeep on a valuable museum acquisition than a real sailor's efforts to make his vessel seaworthy.

As I walked around to the bow of the vessel, I noticed the new white lettering which proclaimed the craft's strange name, the *Black Angel*. A bad omen the name seemed to me. Like many people who have grown up near the sea and spent a lot of time on boats, I'm secretly a little superstitious when it comes to naming vessels.

I was still trying to decide whether to climb up the rope ladder which hung over the *Black Angel*'s side, when Baxter appeared on deck. He spotted me at once and his face lit up.

"Angela! How wonderful to see you.... I'm just doing a bit of work on the *Angelina* - the *Black Angel*, I mean," he corrected himself. "Want to come aboard?"

I nodded, but didn't move.

"Why the *Black Angel*, Baxter? Why not the *Angelina*?" I called up. "She's an almost exact replica of your great-grandfather's boat, isn't she - so why not the same name?"

"Bad luck to name a vessel after a craft so unlucky as the *Angelina* proved to be. It was because of an old letter I came across in the house, I decided on the *Black Angel*. I liked the paradox implicit in this name, I suppose. One day maybe I'll tell you what went through my mind when I made this choice.... Puzzle them some, don't you think?" he laughed, sounding for a moment like one of the local fishermen and not like the erudite and sophisticated man he'd transformed himself into over the years.

After a pause, Baxter began speaking again, but as if to himself. "When you turned up here all those years ago and Jim brought you over to meet me and my mother I guess I originally paid special attention to you because of your name. Angela and Angelina are similar enough to have seemed a stiking coincidence to the introverted and even superstitious teenager I was. I was tempted then to read something fateful into your presence here." Baxter was silent again.

It was, I realized at once, unlike him to have divulged so much about his personal reveries. I glanced up at him, but he seemed to be looking beyond me.

Baxter, the actor, the charmer, the dreamer, I thought as I waited for him to return to the present. In the clear light from the skylights just above his head and from my unusual perspective, he appeared taller and straighter than usual - an aura of strength about him. Though I supposed this strength was illusionary, or at least psychological rather than physical, its appearance nevertheless left a momentarily powerful impression. And as he stood at the rail of the *Black Angel*, I wondered if he saw himself in the role of his great-grandfather, the stalwart seagoing captain of the *Angelina*.

-17-

The *Black Angel* and her skipper were full of surprises. I was
face to face with the first of them before I'd quite reached the top of
the ladder. Suddenly, I found myself staring into the mouth of a cannon, and, as I stopped to pull myself together I could see three others
- one more on the port side and two on the starboard. Hardly what
you'd expect to see on the deck of a yacht at the beginning of the
twenty-first century.

"Hold on now, Angela." I heard Baxter's steady voice close
above me. "I'll give you a hand over the side. Then I'll let you have the
lowdown on my archaic weaponry and the rest of my treasure trove
here."

I stood on the deck of the *Black Angel* gaping and speechless,
like a tourist, while Baxter began his lecture. Professor-curator-
antequarian-ship's captain ... and something else, more elusive, that I
couldn't put my finger on, had merged in this man who had suddenly
projected himself into a role - or series of roles - I would never have
expected to see my low-keyed friend and neighbor assume. I had

pegged Baxter as computer whiz, prize cook, amateur artist and something of a walking encyclopedia on a multitude of subjects, but I had never envisioned him in these other capacities.

He began by telling me how the cannons, like nearly everything else aboard, were replicas of the *Angelina*'s - and how, like the originals, they could be wheeled back into box-like compartments built into the deck which concealed them when they were not in use. Baxter said he moved them out from time to time to make sure the mechanisms continued to work. I wanted to ask why the *Angelina*, a merchant ship, had needed cannons, but Baxter was not to be interrupted. I realized I would have to save my questions until he'd had his say.

Baxter proceeded to explain that both the *Angelina* and the *Black Angel* were modified Tancook schooners. Then he had to tell me what was so special about Tancook schooners. His great-grandfather, Baxter said, had learned about their unique attributes on his first voyage.

He had been a twelve year old cabin boy on a merchant ship which had foundered in a storm near the entrance to Mahone Bay on Nova Scotia's south shore and been picked up, along with another survivor, by a local fisherman headed back to his home on Ironbound Island. The fisherman's boat was a Tancook schooner, built by friends on the neighboring inner island of Tancook. The boy had been amazed by the way the schooner, despite the high seas, had reached Ironbound without difficulty. There and then the boy had resolved that, when he had his own vessel, it would be modelled on this one.

In the days which followed, the boy had listened avidly to his rescuer's accounts of how Tancook schooners, though built inexpensively for local fishing, were not only exceptionally stable but could outrun the sleekest American and British vessels, built by professional shipbuilders at much greater cost. Even after a day's fishing, and loaded to the gunwales, the Ironbound fisherman had bragged, a Tancook schooner with a good skipper and scarcely any crew could outrun most sailing ships between his home island and Barbados.

Baxter went on to tell me how easy these schooners were to handle. In a pinch, he said, one man could manage alone. He told me how even he had sailed the *Black Angel* single-handed, though he had, he said, been a lot more comfortable when he had had Mac along as crew.

By the time his great-grandfather was twenty, Baxter resumed, he had had his own Tancook schooner - the original *Angelina*. He'd also constructed a ramp, rails and pulley system below his Passamaquoddy home, similar to the one on Ironbound, so that he could easily winch his schooner ashore out of reach of the vagaries of the sea.

"This is it, remodelled and updated somewhat." Baxter pointed out the rails and cables visible through the huge double doors which gave onto the sea. "It really is a nifty device," he added.

I'd never appreciated the attributes of this almost hidden cove before. Never *really* looked at it. I suppose even fishermen have tended to steer clear of a place which, from the bay, appears to be unnavigable. Even viewed from the vantage point of the boathouse, the unmarked channel looks dangerous. Though deep, the passage is extremely narrow, its edges rock-strewn. I was surprised that Baxter even considered manoeuvering his precious schooner through such a treacherous-seeming passageway.

Turning away from the pulley and rails and the secluded cove with its narrow channel, I refocused my attention on the *Angelina*'s deck. "So, coming back to the cannons...," I interjected, "surely they weren't a regular feature of a Tancook schooner...?" My words trailed off. As I spoke I began to wonder about what ordinary seagoing men might sometimes have had to do to protect themselves during the early part of the nineteenth century. Unlike Baxter, I was not a naval historian.

"Well," Baxter said thoughtfully, "any seagoing vessel needed to be armed during the war of 1812, for instance. It was hard - perhaps impossible then - to know friend from foe. Any fishing or merchant ship was in danger of being captured and taken into an alien port at gunpoint as a prize. In those days men and boys weren't safe in their own beds at night. Impressment crews came ashore in the wee hours, broke down doors and dragged off able-bodied males to make up the complement of vessels which had lost men in skirmishes up and down the coast. Even the British navy resorted to this barbaric practice," Baxter went on. "So much for the good old days, eh?"

Baxter proceeded to tell me that by the time his great- grandfather was in his mid-twenties the war was officially over. But since our part of the country continued to be disputed territory for the next twenty-five years, there were lots of skirmishes on land and sea. "The border was not fixed here until 1842, so people with illegal enterprises had a field day trading. And even ordinary citizens sometimes felt obliged to take the law into their own hands. Passamaquoddy Bay was so full of pirates and privateers that even if a captain had legitimate business he had to be able to defend himself. No one else was going to look out for him. Skippers of the few revenue cutters, with hundreds of miles of coastline to patrol, couldn't begin to cope with a fraction of the scams they witnessed or suspected.

"I'm sure that's why great-grandfather opted for the cannons as well as the black hull and the slate-colored sails. Since a dark hull and blue-grey sails are less conspicuous than white ones, a lurking priva- teer might suppose that a vessel which was trying to look inconspicu- ous could be another privateer - consequently an armed vessel. Not a prize to be taken without a fight."

*   *   *

The final part of Baxter's tour and commentary took place in the captain's cabin. His cabin, like the *Angelina*'s, was panelled in butternut. Baxter explained how he had removed the wood from the third floor of his house, where, as he pointed out, no one saw the paneling anyway. That top floor hadn't been used for more than a century.

The cabin was both beautiful to look at and utilitarian. Charts of the Bay of Fundy were pinned on the walls, and alongside the berth was a shelf crammed with reference books and paperbacks. The room, I thought, resembled Baxter's study, though, on a smaller, less elaborate scale.

"This chart was drawn by Captain Owen, laird of Campobello, during his survey of the Bay," Baxter remarked proudly, pointing in his best professorial manner to one of the older charts. "It's an original. A collector's piece."

The only objects I saw which distinguished the *Black Angel* from the *Angelina* were the CD player - and, of course, the Loran-C.

-18-

Early next morning I set off for the island, still thinking about Baxter and his schooner and feeling as if I had been on a voyage into times long past. Baxter had held forth so long on the relative merits of the *Angelina* and the *Black Angel*, and I had been overwhelmed with so many historical facts, that I never did find a chance to ask him questions about the island.

By the time he had finished his lecture, he had begun to look paler than usual. The cough which had plagued him most of the winter began to interrupt his flow of words. He had obviously exhausted himself playing the multiple roles he had assumed to entertain me. This performance too - unlike the one he had put on the night of Jim's birthday party - had been impromptu, thus perhaps more wearing. He had had no chance to prepare for my visit. I was concerned about his health.

*   *   *

When I started for the island the sky was clear, the wind steady from the north. As I looked back at the vanishing landscape, the predominant color was green. Despite the cold, everything in Nature was burgeoning. New shoots of grass had emerged from beneath the winter's brown; a green haze emanated from trees and shrubs. Earlier, in the protected dooryard I had noticed that the crocuses were already finished, their translucent white, purple and yellow flowers collapsed and shrinking on the warming earth.

On the bay several other boats were already out and about, though it was just after six. A lone sailboat was visible at the horizon, white sails skimming gull-like between blue sky and bluer water.

For anyone robust enough to cope with the chilling wind, the day was excellent for sailing. Too bad, I thought, that Baxter wasn't up to going out in such weather. Once out on the bay in a schooner like his, it would be easy to imagine oneself back in another era. Construction has altered parts of the coast, but nothing has changed the sea. Not visibly. Not yet. Even in the fishing boat I sensed the timelessness of this enduring element, an easeful sense of past and present merging in wind and wave.

It was time, I knew, to stop fretting about Baxter. I had a full day before me. Besides, I told myself, nearly everything had its flip side. Many of the qualities I found so fascinating and endearing in Baxter stemmed, in all likelihood, from his poor health. Had he been as robust as his forebears or most of the other men who had been at his party, he would almost certainly have been less introspective, less compassionate, less original, less perspicacious - more focused too on the present than on the past. He would not have been the Baxter I was so drawn to.

My speculations about Baxter seemed to have shortened my journey to the island, distancing my concern about what I might find there. As I cut the motor and anchored off the gravel bar, I was cheered to note that nothing appeared to be amiss.

Inkerman was trembling with anxiety to go ashore. Contrary to the widespread Maritime assumption that Labradors are fishermen's dogs, very much at home on the water, Inkerman dislikes boats in general and, I'm convinced, only comes on boating expeditions with me because of the company and the romp once we're on dry land again. He particularly despises choppy weather, when the boat bumps from one wave to another and sometimes dips into troughs from which he cannot apparently imagine it resurfacing. Until we entered the cove he was the picture of dejection.

"What a dog!" I said to him laughing. He wagged his tail tentatively.

It was Jen who was undaunted by the vessel's bumps and grinds, her seeming descent into the depths. She jumped up to be patted, jealous, I suppose, that I'd spoken to Inkerman and not to her - ready to show me that she was game for whatever.... "Brave dog, Jen," I told her as she lay down on my foot. She was in no hurry to disembark as long as water still covered the gravel bar.

Because of the onshore wind, the tide took longer than usual to retreat from the cove. As any fisherman knows, tides can vary somewhat from the heights predicted on the charts, depending on the strength and direction of the wind.

The cove was calm as usual. I collected my gear while I waited for the bar to reappear.

"Just don't forget the sandwiches," Jim always said when he accompanied me on these ventures. Smiling to myself, thinking of Jim, wishing he were present, I stuffed my lunch into the top of my smallest knapsack - the one I wouldn't put down during my walk. Spotty Dotty was not going to share my sandwiches this time.

-19-

I spent a wonderful morning on the island with Inkerman and Jen, finding nothing to trouble me. The sheep all appeared to be well, no dangerous-looking debris had washed ashore, and, best of all, there was no sign of intruders at the spring or elsewhere. The sun continued to shine, and, in places protected from the wind, the earth and even the rocks were warm. I ate my lunch in one of these nooks and was thankful for the day's perfection - so lulled indeed by Nature's beneficent mood that I promptly fell asleep in my hollow near the spring. Not too surprising really: I'd been up and busy since five that morning.

"When things are going well, watch out!" I woke with these words of my Irish grandmother resounding in my head. It was as if she'd spoken them loudly, intending to awaken me. And, although she has been dead for the better part of fifteen years, I sat up and looked around me apprehensively. The warning had the same effect on my good spirits now as similar admonitions had had on the ten year old I'd been. Then my exuberance, exploding on a day like this, had gotten on her nerves and she had dampened it with her dreary superstitious pronouncement.

I shivered, banishing the voice and its message, but still not quite able to rid myself of the unsettling awareness I'd had of her presence - of straining for her words, which were all but drowned out by the soughing of the wind in the treetops and the pounding of waves on the shore.

I quickly dislodged myself from my protected nook and followed the course of the spring's runoff the few hundred feet to the cliff edge. What a sight! I stood there in the wind - a gale really - incredulous, watching the turmoil of the waves. The fury with which they pounded the cliffs was deafening. I wondered how long this had been going on and why I hadn't wakened sooner.

I looked at the sky, which was now overcast, then at my watch. I had been asleep for almost two hours. But even if I had been awake, there was nothing I could have done. The tide was nowhere near right for getting off the island. With such a storm, so much turbulence, and no sign of its letting up, I could see I was going to be marooned on the island for as long as it took for the gale to blow itself out.

This storm had not been predicted. Before setting out I had listened as usual to the marine forecast. There had been nothing ominous in it.

I started back across the island to the cove. Inkerman and Jen, who, like me, had fallen asleep in the sheltered nook, bounded forward, reenergized and exuberant. On reaching the edge of the orchard above the old farmhouse site, I stopped awestruck. The view before me was spectacular.

The cove, guarded by the massive encircling arms of stone, was as tranquil as ever, the *Bay Lady* riding safely at anchor. But, outside this haven, Pandemonium ruled. Gigantic waves rose and broke against the rock face, sending spray high into the air. And, off to the left, the exposed tidal rip between our island and its neighbor - some half mile away - looked uglier and more treacherous than ever. Heaven help a boat caught there any day at the wrong time! But on a day like this, it seemed as if nothing could save a hapless mariner from a watery grave. It was not the sort of weather anyone could put out in. You'd never make it out of the cove without being dashed to smithereens on the rocks.

I thanked my lucky stars for being safe on shore, even if the situation wasn't the one I would have chosen. In my elevated and exposed position, the wind was icy. Even with my jacket tightly zipped up, I still felt chilled to the marrow. I shivered and thought of my sleeping bag, the pup tent and emergency supplies stashed in the locker of the *Bay Lady*. I'd have to take the row boat and go after them before I got much older. Although I had always carried these things for just such and eventuality, this was the first time I had had to use them. Even though I knew how unpredictable the Bay of Fundy weather could be, it was still hard to believe that so violent a storm had come up so suddenly.

I shivered again, and found that I was now shaking uncontrollably - partly from the icy wind and freezing rain which had just begun, and partly, I supposed, from my uneasiness about the situation in which I found myself. What if this gale kept up? What if it blew for days? I could not get off the island and no one could get out to me as long as it lasted.

Then I thought of the cave. I could find shelter there. I could light the kerosene stove I had seen there, cook up a meal, sleep on a cot. I consoled myself with the assurance that the owners of this paraphernalia could no more get onto the island than I could get off - unless, of course, they were already holed up in the cave, having come in on the Zodiac before my arrival.

I decided to check out the hideaway discretely before I ventured in. I wasn't sure whether that was possible but I knew I would have to chance it. Even if the hideaway was unoccupied I would have to keep a close watch on the weather, be ready to leave on the first tide, once the wind dropped.

-20-

I rowed out to the *Bay Lady* for gear and food - flashlight, sleeping bag, dog food, canned beans, soup packages, powdered milk and eggs, dried fruit and hardtack - the traditional ship's biscuits - thanking my lucky stars all the while that this natural harbor was so protected and Vernon so farsighted as to leave the old rowboat on the shore for just such an emergency as this. Whether I had to camp out or hole up in the cave, I'd need all, or most of these - the pup tent too, if I opted to stay outside. But I found myself counting on occupying the cave, getting out of the wind and wet and making myself as comfortable as possible before nightfall. I willed the interlopers not to be there.

* * *

When I yanked open the root cellar door and peered down, everything, as far as I could tell, looked as before. But just to make sure the coast was clear, I invited Jen and Inkerman down the steps, sure that Inkerman anyway would warn me if he sensed that anyone was in the cave. Flashlight in hand, I picked my way along the passageway.

Inkerman pressed forward, unperturbed. Gingerly, I pulled the rope which Inkerman had tugged on our last visit. As before, the wooden back of the root cellar swung aside and the cave was exposed.

Fortunately, the cave was untenanted.

After dropping my knapsack inside the cave, just at the bottom of the stone steps, I looked around carefully to determine what else I might need that I had forgotten to bring from the boat. To light the kerosene heater and the camp stove, I needed matches. A box lay on the table.

The only other thing I could think of which I would need but didn't have was water. I would have to refill my thermos jug at the spring. Everything else - dishes and cutlery, as well as several small saucepans - were all neatly stacked on a shelf near the camp stove.

I picked the thermos up and turned to leave when I decided to check the matchbox on the table. No point in waiting till it was dark to find out that the box was empty. It was, however, full, and I was just turning away from the table when I thought of Jim's knife - or the one resembling it - which I had seen lying there on my former visit. Not a sign of it now. Who had pocketed it?

Wondering about this unknown person, I felt sick, terrified, trapped. What if he - or they - caught me here? Anyone could kill me in this place with impunity. There was little likelihood of my body being discovered. And if I was thrown into the sea, my demise would be put down as an accident.

That was when I noticed that the platform on which the Zodiac had rested was empty.

I tried to pull myself together, persuading myself back to sanity by my recollection of a raging sea, the rip between the islands, the gale force winds. So long as the storm lasted, this place was *my* fortress, *my* sanctuary. No one could come ashore in such a storm. I was safe until the weather and tide changed.

*   *   *

Inkerman, Jen and I set off for the spring. The rain which had begun just before I set out to the *Bay Lady* for supplies was now mixed with snow. I was terribly chilled. The uncertainty of my situation had made me tense, less resistant than usual to the cold.

-21-

Once I'd got the water, establishing myself in the cave was easy. I lit the kerosene heater, the camp stove and two of the oil lamps - one on the table, the other in a wall niche. While I waited for the kettle to boil, I fed the dogs their dry rations. Soup and tea, as well as crackers and cheese left over from lunch would do me for supper, I decided.

Having eaten, Inkerman lay down with a sigh of contentment beside my gear, his head resting on my knapsack. Jen sat watchfully at the foot of the stone steps, her food untouched. She hadn't decided what she thought of being shut up in a cave with Inkerman and me. She is used to sleeping in her kennel in the barn and eating in privacy.

The cave soon became comfortable, the heater taking off the damp which had seeped up from below. Although the platform on which the Zodiac had rested shut the lower cave off from the upper one where I sat, dampness seeped in around the cracks. The heater was necessary to dry things out.

While I ate my supper, I listened to the tremendous swishing, pounding and gurgling going on beneath the Zodiac platform, indicating that the tide was high. The steady pulsing was hypnotic. Suddenly feeling overpoweringly sleepy, I extinguished the table lamp, took my cup of tea over to the cot, climbed into my sleeping bag, and, lulled by the strong and regular tempo of the surging waves, promptly fell asleep.

* * *

I must have slept five or six hours. When I awoke, the lamp in the wall niche was still burning, throwing an eerie and trembling light in its immediate vicinity. The noisy slooshing-gurgling-beating which had been going on below when I had fallen asleep had stopped. The tide was out. I wondered if the storm had blown itself out, or whether I simply couldn't tell because of the thickness of the cave walls and ceiling.

I had to know. Climbing out of my sleeping bag and grabbing the flashlight, I yanked open the panel leading into the root cellar and hurried down the passageway to the trap door entrance. I told the dogs to stay.

The storm still raged. No need to climb up the outer steps to feel its violence. I had not pulled the trap door down after me when I had entered the passageway because I thought I mightn't be able to push it up from the inside. Consequently, I was exposed to the elements as soon as I got to the bottom of the steps leading up into the blackberry patch. Wet snow and rain beat down on me, and, when I climbed part way up the stairs, the wind tore at my hair. Since it was still too dark to see anything, I retreated thankfully to the cave and lay down again on the cot.

Wide awake after my sleep and foray into the fresh air, I looked around curiously at what I could see of my strange surroundings. Since this was very little, except in the immediate vicinity of the light from the niche lamp, I soon found myself scrutinizing the stone face near the light.

The color of the rock was variegated - the indentations irregular. Although I had thought that the cave walls were grey, I saw that they were actually blue-grey, shading into a dusty rose. In the niche behind the lamp, I observed fissures which formed a rectangle of such regularity that it looked as if it had been cut into the stone with a precision instrument. I turned my head from side to side, willing the cracks to disappear so that I could see that they were optical illusions produced by the uncertain light. But, whichever way I moved, the outline of the rectangle remained.

At length, unable to focus on anything else, I got up and stood beside the lamp. But from close up the glare blinded me. I could see nothing in the niche behind it.

I tried to lift the lamp down, but it appeared to be anchored. Then I felt around behind the lamp, hoping to locate whatever was holding it. As I reached back into the niche, my fingers encountered a knob which was not quite flush with the stone. It felt metallic.

I wiggled it a little and then found I could turn it. When I did, the stone behind the lamp receded.

I felt an opening, but could not see it. The light from the wall lamp, instead of illuminating the space behind it, simply shone in my eyes, preventing my seeing what lay beyond.... I had to know what was there.

Trembling with curiosity, excitement and impatience, I relit the table lamp, returned to the wall niche with my flashlight, turned down the niche lamp, removed its glass chimney and blew out the still remaining glimmer. Now my flashlight revealed a rectangular opening which in size corresponded to the outline of the cracks I had seen earlier from the cot. This cubbyhole appeared to be a primitive and diminutive wall safe. It was stacked with papers.

With great care I removed about half the papers - the top seven or eight inches - laying them on the table. But where my hands had grasped the bundle, the brownish edges had crumbled and fallen to the cave floor in fragments as unrecoverable as those wafted from a fire. Whatever they were, it was apparent that these hand-written pages had not been touched for a great many years. Whoever had recently rediscovered the cave had not found this hiding place.

Shining my flashlight back into the 'safe', I could see that beneath the remaining pile of papers there appeared to be several books. Carefully, I eased these leather-bound volumes out from under the papers. I did not contemplate untying the loose pages until I could figure out some way of doing this without destroying them.

My thesis researches had yielded no material so fragile. I could better understand now, though, why librarians were so reluctant to let researchers touch original old documents, and consequently why microfilming was so crucial.

The leather-bound volumes, three in all, seemed less fragile than the loose pages. Slowly I turned back the cover of the uppermost and read at the top of the page

Log of the Angelina III

written in a neat and regular hand. Inscribed immediately below were the date and location

January 1 1842   Boston

This log, I realized, must have been taken from Baxter's great grandfather's schooner and secreted here. The questions were: When? ... By whom? Under what circumstances?

In my excitement, I almost forgot my own predicament. Uppermost in my mind was my longing for Baxter to be here, to share the thrill of this recent discovery and help solve the mysterious circumstances surrounding the contemporary users of the cave. Keeping all my recent finds to myself and not being able to figure out how the facts fitted together was becoming too much of a burden. Too dangerous as well.

I resolved to tell Baxter all I had discovered as soon as I got home. Meanwhile, I idly turned over the pages in the logbook before me.

A newspaper clipping caught my eye. The diary entry had been obscured by the clipping which had adhered to the diary page. The caption proclaimed that the paper was the *Weekly Chronicle*, Saint John, New Brunswick, January 7, 1842. Someone had placed a cross beside two of the items - FALSE LIGHTS and notes on vessels which followed the SHIPPING LIST. The column marked was in small print, wedged in amidst advertisements in larger print: "Old London Particular Madeira; fine old Pale Brandy, vintage of 1835, and 1838; 100 puncheons RUM - Old Jamaica, Demerara, and Cuba - some 80 per cent O.P.; 100 chests Souchong TEA; 100 Boxes Candles and Soap; 10 casks superior French VINEGAR; a few dozen Loaf Cheddar Cheese; 400 Kegs London White Lead, Black, Red, and Yellow Paint; and 100 Cans GREEN PAINT."

I read both of the marked items without being able to determine their significance.

FALSE LIGHTS - Captain Loring, of packet schr. Mail, from New-York arrived 22d inst states that on Saturday night last, when off Cape Elizabeth Island, between Quix's Hole and Cutterhunk Light, he discovered a bright light and supposed it to be Tarpaulin Cove Light, stood accordingly, when suddenly the light disappeared, and he discovered that he was standing in among breakers. The wind was blowing freshly and he had barely time to go about in time to save his vessel. The schr. Benj. Bigelow, also from New-York, passed the same place a few hours afterwards, and was decoyed by the same light, and came near going ashore.-*Boston Courier.*

* * *

Ship Wallace, which went ashore on the ledges off Grand Manan, on the 23d of May last, on her passage from Liverpool to this port, laden with a valuable cargo, and which, after much expenditure in endeavours to raise her, was finally abandoned, has been driven by the late gales and heavy sea, into Seal Cove, Grand Manan; and now in 24 feet of water - much of her cargo remains in her; and it is expected a large quantity, consisting of copper, iron, &c., will be got out without material damage.

Ship William, Capt. Foster, of and from Liverpool, for this port, out 32 days, with iron, earthenware, &c. was totally lost on Bell Rock, near Ragged Island, Nova Scotia, on the 19th ult.-Two of the crew drowned. Part of the crew arrived here yesterday morning in the schooner Hare from Digby.

Spoken, Dec. 20, lat 39 40 long 69 40, barque Henry Hood, from Boston for Savannah.

Schr. James Clark, at this port 22d, from St. John, N.B. was last from Boothbay, where she put in with loss of foremast in the gale of 14th inst.-*Boston Paper.*

Schr. Sussex, Capt. Harris, of and for Westport from Antigua, on the 4th ult. lat 38 40, long. 55 30, fell in with the wreck of the schr. Fame, Capt. Foster, of Port Medway, capsized and dismasted, and took from her Capt. F. and crew, who had been four days on the wreck, with scarcely any nourishment. Two hours after being taken off, a heavy gale commenced. The mate of the F., Mr. Williams, died on the 8th. The R. was capsized in a gale on the 30th Nov.-*Yarmouth Her. Dec. 24.*

Ship Odessa, Vaughan, of St. John, 61 days from Glasgow, bound to New York, with 153 passengers, put into Barrington, on the 14th inst. short of provisions and water.-*Ibid.*

* * *

I closed the log book and put it aside, resolved to take it home with me and see what Baxter and I could make of it and the newspaper clippings. I opened the second book. It too was a log of the *Angelina 111* - for part of 1841. A cursory examination of this log indicated that it was nothing more than a daily record of the vessel's position and progress, the weather, other vessels sighted and any irregularities having to do with the crew's behavior. I saw no clippings, though I found the elaborate menu from a Boston hotel lodged between the mid-September entries.

Despite what Baxter had told me about the original *Angelina* being designed, like his own, to handle easily - with very few hands, if necessary - it appeared from a random examination of the log that the *Angelina III* had had a crew of four or five, in addition to master, mate and cook.

From marginal jottings, it was clear the captain had brought his young wife on one of the voyages recorded in this book. Here and there were comments such as "Maggie ill again today.... Maggie with child.... M. too young a lass for a venture such as this."

Such as what? I wondered.... "Too young as well for a man my age," I read on, and then closed the log after reading: "M. on at me again about Angelina.... Both A. herself and naming my schooners after her."

Placing this second volume alongside the first, I decided to take it home along with the other.

The third volume I at first assumed was another log book, though its cover differed from the others. It had at one time been secured by a metal clasp and locked, but the lock and clasp were broken, as if the lock had been forced. I flipped open the cover and realized that this was a diary written in the same neat and regular hand as the logs. It would provide answers, I hoped, to some of the many questions which had begun to flood my mind.

But perusing them would have to wait until I was safe at my own kitchen table or with Baxter in his study. I put the three books in my knapsack, filling the void which had been left there when I removed the food. Then I replaced the loose papers - documents, or whatever they were - gently in the vault and pulled the stone door to by the protruding knob. The rectangular stone moved easily into place, and, if I had not had some of the evidence with me, I would have suspected I had been dreaming. Nothing so peculiar had happened to me ever before. This was, I told myself, a first-rate example of fact being stranger than fiction.

I bent over to sweep up the paper fragments, and began to look around for any other telltale signs of my presence in the cave. If the men who used this place as a hideaway learned that someone else had discovered it, they would, I felt sure, take whatever steps were necessary to find out who had been in the cave. How they would deal with such an intruder didn't bear thinking about.

-22-

By mid-morning the following day the storm had blown itself out, and, by evening, I was back in my own kitchen, warming up leftover meat loaf and scalloped potatoes. I took in with new appreciation the familiar objects in the room, feeling like a weary traveller who had returned home after a long absence in foreign lands instead of a local householder who had merely been stranded part way across the bay overnight. Yet rationalize as I might, my overwhelming contentment at being home again approximated no feeling I had known before except the relief of awakening from a particularly horrific nightmare. In fact, if I hadn't had the log books and diary before me on the table, I might have tried to put the events of the past two days out of my mind. Pretend they hadn't happened. I really didn't want to deal with them and I had no idea where to begin.

* * *

I had just finished supper when Vernon and Martha dropped

by. They were so eager to bring me up to date on the damage the storm had caused along the coast that they did not at once inquire about my doings.

By the time Martha got round to saying, "And so, my dear, tell us what you've been doing with yourself the last couple of days," I found myself hesitating briefly and then replying with somewhat forced casualness.

"Oh, this and that. Not much. Just puttering around.... The usual..."

Although I was eager to confide in someone, I still couldn't bring myself to explain. Tomorrow, early, I promised myself I would unburden myself to Baxter - tomorrow, after I had had a good sleep in my own bed and another look at the volumes I had brought home.

But that was not to be. Jim came by just as Martha and Vernon were leaving to invite me to a party on Saturday night at Chester's. "We all took turns calling you yesterday but no one could get you. Why don't you answer your phone?"

Tempted as I was I didn't try to explain. Actually, the more complicated the whole business became, the less able I felt to talk about it.

*   *   *

More than half the people who had been at Baxter's do for Jim's birthday were at Chester's. The mood, however, was altogether different. As Howard observed more than once in his usual obnoxious way, "There's no way anyone can match Baxter's grub." The difference, though, was not just the food.

I looked around for Baxter. When I couldn't see him I decided to ask Chester where he was.

Chester's explanations were always short and to the point. He isn't a talker, but that night he had more to say than usual. "Baxter had last minute company - a guy, maybe two. From New York ... Buffalo... Bangor - somewhere down there. Phoned to say he couldn't come tonight. Something about a new computer."

Chester fell silent then, seemingly preoccupied. 'Glum,' was the word Jim used to describe Chester's expression that night. I put his prevailing gloom and moodiness down to having to spend so much time with Howard and the twins. The latter, though not too bad singly, were incredibly irritating when they got together - which must have seemed all too often to Chester. That evening, the twins, on home ground, were acting sillier than ever. I was sure Chester's wife embarrassed him in public most of the time. Jim had told me privately that he thought the marriage was in trouble, though, as he added, Chester was too loyal to discuss it.

Suddenly I felt overwhelmingly weary. I looked around for Jim. He had brought me and I wanted to ask him to take me home. I didn't think I could stand a long evening of Howard's wisecracks, Chester's gloom and the twins' inane behavior. Apparently Jim had been feeling the same way, and we came together in unanimous accord.

"I'm going to tell Chester I'm done in after that last week on the road," Jim confided. "That's true, by the way.... Ches is an understanding kind of guy.

"Anyhow, I want to talk to Baxter. Can we go by there on the way home, or do you want me to drop you off first?

"Maybe those computer guys won't stay long and I can ask Baxter a couple of questions that have been driving me nuts. It shouldn't take long."

-23-

All the lights were on in Baxter's house. Surprising! They blazed out across the yard so that, despite the darkness of the night, the drive-way within twenty feet of the house was clearly lit.

The bright overhead lights in the hall and living room, which Baxter never used, were on. He once told me that he thought them too harsh, unflattering to the room and the people in it. Except in the kitchen, or directly over his desk when he was working, Baxter kept his lights so dim that Jim used to kid him that, on a dark night, he couldn't see across any of his rooms, couldn't tell who or what might be lurking in the hidden corners. Even on the night of Jim's birthday party only the downstairs table lamps and the dresser lamp in the upstairs master bedroom had been on.

So we were somewhat apprehensive - puzzled anyway. Jim tried to make fun of our fears, but for once his kidding was half-hearted.

There was no car in the driveway except Baxter's. His visitors had apparently driven off in a hurry. There were tire burns on the lawn close to the front door where someone had turned hastily, not taking time to back onto the gravelled ramp.

We knocked at the door, but I think by then neither of us expected an answer because we didn't wait. The door wasn't locked, so we walked in, Jim calling Baxter's name. There was no response.

The big front hall looked as usual, but the living room had been vandalized. The coffee table was overturned, the end tables too and the contents of their drawers spewed across the room. The floor lamp had been knocked over, its shade trampled. Broken pieces of the miniature *Angelina* littered the hearth. Someone had swept candlesticks, model ship, even the packs of cigarettes off the mantle and onto the stonework.

Jim turned back into the hall and yanked open the study door. Worse devastation was apparent here. The chaos and breakages in the living room were nothing by comparison. Almost everything in the study appeared to have been shaken loose as if by a violent earthquake. Books had been toppled from shelves, chairs and lamps smashed, the desk drawers emptied and apparently hurled across the room. The only piece of furniture which remained upright and in its usual position was Baxter's massive oak desk. The vandals must have found it too heavy to upend. Surprisingly, the computer had not been smashed. In the midst of the upheaval its screen was bright.

It was not until Jim and I moved around the desk to see what was on the computer screen, hoping that it might give us a clue as to what this was all about, that we saw Baxter's feet and legs protruding from beneath a heap of books and papers. His head and torso were wedged beneath the desk. He showed no sign of life. I began to cry.

Jim was down on his knees at once, his head poked under the desk close to Baxter's. He pulled back after an instant and looked up at me. "Oh, come on, Angela. You sound like a baby. And don't look so hopeless. He's out cold, but he's not dead, for Christ's sake. Come on, give me a hand moving these books, and then we'll pull him out from under here."

Clearing away the books and papers didn't take long, but I balked at the idea of pulling Baxter out from under the desk. Admonitions I'd read about not moving an injured person until you know what's wrong with him jumped to mind.

My hesitancy exasperated Jim. He turned on me."Well, how the hell do you know what's the matter with somebody who's in a position like this until you get them out where you can have a look?" Jim was not his usual laid-back self.

"Moving him could kill him," I said tentatively, still afraid that Baxter, if not indeed dead, might be close to death. And then I lost my temper, something I rarely do. Trying to cope with this terrible and incomprehensible violence on top of all the other frightening events of the past forty-eight hours suddenly overwhelmed me. I felt exhausted, wrung out. I needed to sleep to restore my equilibrium. But that wasn't possible. Jim and I had to save Baxter and do something about this mess.

"Well, don't just stand there," I snarled. "Do something. Call the ambulance. Call the police. Call the doctor..." I couldn't believe that such an out-of-control and disagreeable voice was mine.

"Can't," Jim interrupted, calm and matter-of-fact now that he thought I was going to pieces. "Look at the phone wire. It's been cut. I'll have to go for help."

Our voices must have roused Baxter. He stirred and sighed faintly.

"He is coming to," Jim and I blurted out simultaneously.

"Baxter, old man, tell us where you're hurt.... Come on now...." Jim was on his knees, his head in the leg space between the drawers so that he could hear whatever Baxter might say. I knelt down beside him.

"Help me ... out...," Baxter whispered, his words followed by a sigh which faded into silence.

Instead of yanking him out from under the desk, feet first, as I could see Jim was still inclined to do, I suggested we try to move the desk back away from Baxter. At first this seemed impossible. The desk is massive and heavy. I guessed it weighed almost as much as a grand piano. However, we persevered. And bit by bit, a fraction of an inch at a time, we pushed the huge desk away from Baxter's inert form leaving ugly gouge lines in the pine floorboards.

After we had eased the desk back about a foot, Jim unplugged the printer and set the computer down gently on a hooked mat near the outlet. The directory was still bluely lit.

"Hang on there, old man, we'll have you into the open in a jiffy... Come on, Angela, just a couple of big heaves. Together... One... two... That's right.... Now we can see what's what."

Seeing what was what was not comforting. A long gash, from hairline to chin ran down the left side of Baxter's face. Because the blood had congealed over it, we couldn't tell how deep it was. His left eye was swollen shut, and the back of his right hand had turned bluish-black. Where his shirt was ripped, the buttons torn off, scratches were visible on his midriff. Any other wounds he might have were hidden by his clothes.

"You'd better go for help, Jim," I said as matter-of-factly as I could. Worried as I was about Baxter, I was also frightened to stay alone in this house after what had happened. Whoever had done this might return. Still, I didn't see any alternative: we needed help.

It was Baxter who stopped Jim from leaving. He was conscious again. "Stay here, Jim," he commanded, faintly, but urgently, making an immense effort to pull himself together.

"No one else must know about this. I've got to get better on my own - if I'm going to get better," Baxter remarked in an ironic after-thought, before subsiding again into that nether world from which he had briefly emerged.

Jim frowned at me over Baxter's inert form, flummoxed by Baxter's apparently totally unreasonable attitude. But we both had so much respect for Baxter's judgement that neither of us argued.

"We'd better get him to my place as fast as possible," I said to

Jim, trying hard now to sound controlled and reasonable. "We can't leave him here and we daren't stay much longer. Suppose whoever did this returns?"

"Well, how are we going to get him out of here? ... You said we shouldn't move him.... And what if we can't fix him up? ... Suppose he's broken a leg or an arm? Suppose his injuries are internal? Looks like he needs a doctor ... x-rays ... tests ... a stay in hospital. The hospital's definitely the place for him right now."

While Jim was spewing out this list of obstacles, Baxter slowly lifted his left arm and then his right. "Not broken," he murmured, sounding surprised. "Can't tell yet about my legs. Help me sit up." He held out his arms like a small child, the eye which wasn't swollen shut open now and peering up at us.

And so we went over Baxter bit by bit without finding anything which seemed to require a doctor's expertise, though it was impossible to tell for certain. After tending animals for so long, I had become a moderately successful makeshift vet, but whatever medical knowledge I had acquired looking after injured sheep and dogs - a donkey too - had never been applied to human beings with serious-seeming problems. It was clear that was about to change.

After easing Baxter into the middle of a queen-sized Hudson's Bay blanket - the strongest material of roughly the right size which we could lay our hands on - Jim and I managed to transport him on this makeshift stretcher to Jim's *Pathfinder.* Baxter kept losing and regaining consciousness during this move. But just as we were about to pull out of the driveway, it was clear that Baxter was trying to tell us something he thought we had to know. He sounded more acutely distressed than he had about his own injuries. What he managed to communicate was that Bruiser had been left behind, shut in the basement by the 'visitors'. Jim ran back into the house, returning seconds later with an unusually sedate and limping dog. Nevertheless, when I held open the vehicle's back door Bruiser was able to jump in and lie down beside his master.

We were both relieved to get out of Baxter's long driveway. Jim, who does not have an overactive imagination like mine, was tense. As he told me later, he half expected to have our way blocked by "those hoods." Since the occurrences at Baxter's house were so extraordinarily bizarre for this quiet rural community where most people still leave their doors unlocked, we had difficulty believing that what had happened was real.

Without any prodding from me, Jim took a roundabout way to my house. "Just in case someone might follow us," Jim explained needlessly. But no one did. We saw only two vehicles, a half ton and a transport, both of which passed us at high speeds going in the opposite direction.

The lights were off in the few houses we passed. It was after 2 a.m.

Jim began to relax. I couldn't. He looked across at me and put his hand on my arm. "Lighten up, little cousin. I'll bet those hoods are all snug in their jammies by now. Even thugs need to sleep."

Jim's good at relieving tense situations, though this one must have taxed his powers of invention. Anyhow, his quips must have helped. Both of us yawned at once, exhausted now that the adrenalin had stopped flowing. Baxter had fallen asleep as soon as we had left his driveway. He scarcely stirred even when we carried him into my house and put him to bed in the spare bedroom.

-24-

A persistent whining woke me early the next morning. Only half conscious, my eyes still closed, I murmured sleepily, "Well, what's the matter with you, old boy? Hush now...."

The whining continued and I was hazily conscious that some-thing had to be amiss: it wasn't like Inkerman to fuss so. But when I opened my eyes, it was Bruiser, not Inkerman, who was staring down at me. He wagged his tail and frowned, appearing at once pleased to have got my attention and apologetic about having disturbed me.

Suddenly the events of the preceding evening came rushing back to me and I jumped out of bed wondering how, under such unsettling circumstances, I could possibly have slept so soundly. I had intended to check on Baxter every hour at least. Instead, I had lost conscious-ness for who knew how long. I wondered if Baxter had called out for me, needing help. At least, I comforted myself as I scurried down the hall, I had had the wit to station Bruiser beside Baxter's bed and he had come to tell me I was needed.

When I asked Baxter how he was, he answered at once, his

voice sounding stronger than it had when Jim and I had put him to bed. But he still looked a mess - perhaps even worse than when we had found him - and I wondered why Jim and I had ever agreed to Baxter's plea not to take him to the hospital and not to contact the police. The swollen eye looked more distended, and into the dominant black and blue a horrid greenish yellow had crept. Surprisingly, though, the gash had already begun to close and heal. Before cleaning off the blood the preceding night, I had thought that it might need stitches, but, though the slash was long, it had proved to be thin and superficial - made, Jim had guessed, by a knife with a very fine, razor-sharp edge.

Baxter tried to smile at me in the lopsided, self-conscious way someone does who has just been to the dentist and still has one side of his mouth frozen. He asked if I would mind making him some porridge - runny in consistency so that it would slide down easily. By suppertime, he'd added, he would try to be up and around. If Baxter was already thinking about food, I consoled myself, there was an indication that he might be on the mend.

*   *   *

Although Baxter wasn't up for supper that night, and his recovery proceeded slowly, he nevertheless improved visibly over the next couple of days. Jim took two days off work "to help with the nursing," he said. And although he was little help in that department, he provided both Baxter and me with lots of moral support and even a few laughs. As well, that first morning, he had gone over to the old house "to reconnoiter," he said.

He came back disgruntled, saying that he hadn't found any clues. However, as I pointed out, this was his first stint playing detective: he couldn't expect to be a pro overnight.

But he said he wasn't keen on poking around the scene of a crime, that he wanted to call in the authorities, put the whole nasty business in someone else's hands. He didn't approve, he said, of

Baxter's insistence that we keep the police out of this.

Although Baxter improved rapidly - more quickly than we expected, given his never very robust health - he remained tight-lipped about what had happened before we rescued him. And when two days went by without Baxter even alluding to the attack, Jim was exasperated. I found Baxter's silence easier to relate to after having nursed my own troublesome secrets for more than a week.

Still it was clear that such an awkward situation couldn't go on. So, on the afternoon of the third day after the attack, when Jim had returned to work, I resolved to bring everything out in the open. Not knowing how to begin, I decided that, instead of quizzing Baxter about what had occurred at his house, I would tell him about my island experiences as I had long intended. I wasn't sure if I would tell him everything. What I said would depend on his response. I planned to begin by giving him his great-grandfather's papers. He had a right to them. Perhaps if he looked at them, this voice from the past together with my story would elicit a response and an explanation.

-25-

Before tackling Baxter, I settled him in a deck chair on the porch, hoping that the sun, the fresh air and the spectacular view would do him good - "bring him out of himself," as my grandmother would have said. The screens would protect him from mosquitoes and black flies, the roof from too much sun. He could watch the fishermen tending their weirs offshore in the distance, almost directly across from where he sat. Bruiser, lying at his side, would provide undemanding company. The prospect seemed ideal.

I went back into the house for the diary and the two log books and, on returning, set them down carefully on the table beside Baxter. "Here, have a look at these," I said, my tone demanding, I hoped, rather than suggesting. I was determined to have him listen to me, to break through the wall he had been building around himself since the attack. "They should interest you. They're your great-grandfather's," I said bluntly, not looking directly at him, not wanting to be disappointed if he failed to respond. Then, without waiting for an answer, I rambled on. "That means, of course, that they really belong to you. I haven't read them yet, haven't had time, though I did glance at a few pages. The logs are from the *Angelina* - not the first *Angelina*, but the third. Did you know there was more than one?" Again, I didn't wait for an answer. As I turned away, ready to retreat to the kitchen, I told Baxter that I was going to make supper and that, once I had the casseroles in the oven, I'd be back. "Then we'll talk," I said. "I have to tell you how I came by your great-grandfather's papers.

"Like you, I've had a terrifying experience, one I don't know how to deal with. I don't know who to turn to - who I can trust to keep a secret - except you."

*   *   *

When I returned almost an hour later, Baxter was alert and watchful. And, although the detachment of the past few days had vanished, the struggle he had obviously undergone to pull himself together showed in a more intense pallor than before. A brief glance at him made me wish I'd let him be, allowed him to recover before presenting him with the log books and diary. But it was too late now to backtrack.

As soon as I sat down, Baxter began to speak. Looking at me directly and sounding almost normal, he said, "Angela, you've got to tell me how you came by these."

"Oh, the old books," I said, stalling for time, suddenly uncertain about how to proceed. I wished that Baxter looked more his old self - had seemed more cheerful and less ill.

But since I am not much good at beating around the bush, I came right out with the answer. "On Sheep Island - four days ago," I replied, sounding, I thought, as if I felt that the island was the most normal place in the world to find old manuscripts.

"On Sheep Island?" Baxter sounded suitably incredulous. If Baxter had been feeling himself, I would have teased him, pleased with the effect of surprising him. But the light-hearted repartee we usually engage in was clearly inappropriate.

"In a cave I stumbled into," I replied, trying to sound matter of fact.

Baxter's reply, though fitting in with some of my conjectures about his finding the cave in the course of childhood adventures with Jim, Lyle and Mac nevertheless took me aback. "So you've found the cave," he said. "How?... Tell me about it." He was concentrating all his attention on me now, awaiting my reply.

*   *   *

Quickly, I spilled out everything that had happened on the island: how I had retrieved the cigarette pack beside the cliff path and seen the footstep near the spring; how later I had found the root cellar accidentally because of Spotty Dotty's daughter accidentally catching her leg in the ring which opened the trap door; how, when I had gone down to investigate, Inkerman had tugged on the rope loop so that the panel had swung back exposing the cave; how that first time in the cave I had seen the Zodiac, the piled boxes, which I had supposed were filled with cartons of cigarettes, and the knife resembling Jim's on the table; and finally how, on being stranded on the island during the storm, I had taken shelter in the cave.

I digressed a little here to tell Baxter about the storm. I described the wildness of the sea, the contrasting calmness of the protected cove and the terrors of the tidal rip between the islands at the turn of the tide. He was as good a listener as I had hoped, nodding sympathetically at the appropriate moments, attending closely. Just the confidant I'd needed.

When I related how I had discovered the 'wall safe' behind the niche and found the log books and diary inside, he leaned forward eagerly, his eyes alight with enthusiasm, the way they'd been the day he'd given me the tour of the *Black Angel*. I even told him about the crumbling papers I had left behind because of their extraordinary fragility.

Recounting all this took longer than I had expected, and I was just preparing to listen to what Baxter had to say when Jim turned into the driveway. As soon as he stepped onto the porch I could see that he sensed the changed mood. He could see that we had been talking and smell the good dinner in the offing. He smiled down at both of us, obviously cheered.

"So, old fellow," Jim said, sitting down beside Baxter, "how're things?"

I'm always grateful for Jim's good nature and diplomacy. Although he was clearly relieved that Baxter was himself again and curious about the conversation he had come in on, he had the good grace not to probe. Although he's not good at keeping secrets, he does have a sixth sense sometimes about knowing when to bide his time, to pick neutral topics of conversation at difficult moments.

"I can see Angela's been talking your ear off. I suppose she's been entertaining you with some of the local gossip."

"Well, something like that," Baxter rejoined noncommitally. "It's true, I've hardly been able to get a word in edgeways...." He smiled at us both.

Jim looked surprised. On observing our tête-à-tête, it would have been natural for him to assume that Baxter had been explaining about the night he was attacked. Baxter was not slow to pick up on Jim's unspoken questions.

"After supper," he said promptly, "I'll fill you in about what happened to me the other night. I'm sorry I've kept you both in the dark these last couple of days, but I couldn't seem to pull myself together enough to discuss the whole strange business. It was such a shock."

-26-

Baxter told us that he had been about to set off for Chester's party when the telephone had begun ringing and he had answered it. The caller had identified himself at once as a distant and long-lost cousin. Rollie Brooks, he'd called himself. He said he had to see Baxter at once on urgent family business.

Baxter had laughed and hung up, convinced that the unfamiliar voice was one of Lyle's impersonations, staged to entertain the early arrivals at Chester's party.

"I can see how you came to that conclusion," Jim interjected, smiling. Then, turning to me, he explained what he meant. "When we were kids, Lyle and I - some of the others too - were always joking around about turning over our excess relatives - the ones we didn't particularly like - to Baxter to make up for his total, and to us incomprehensible, lack of aunts, uncles, cousins, brothers and sisters. We never seemed to get over our amazement that he didn't have a super-abundance of relations like the rest of us. Still haven't, I guess."

"Before I had time to leave the front hall," Baxter resumed, "the phone rang again. The voice was obviously the previous caller's, but the tone had become peremptory."

"My great-grandfather and yours were cousins," the caller announced hurriedly, seeming determined to get in his two cents worth this time before being cut off again. "I've got some pretty fascinating documents with me to prove it.... Be there in a jiffy."

The caller had hung up without waiting for a reply, and, before Baxter had decided how to react, someone was ringing his front doorbell.

"To get here so soon that 'long-lost cousin' must have called from a cell phone in my driveway," Baxter said he had recalled thinking as he opened the door.

He had been annoyed but not suspicious, certainly not apprehensive. Unwanted visitors in these parts might be intrusive, boring people half to death, but they had never been known to harm anyone.

"Brooks?" Baxter remembered saying to the man, but looking more closely at the wooden box than at the man holding it.

"Yes, that's me. Where can we go to take the weight off of our feet?" he had said impatiently, looking around for a spot which suited him and obviously not finding one in the front hall. "Carrying this box is a pain anywhere you like to mention."

Baxter said he'd glanced down at the man then and concluded in a brief survey that he seemed to be cut off the same pattern as Howard. Short. Overweight. Sandy hair, merging into skin of much the same color. Nondescript features, sunk in pudginess. An aggressive manner. A smart aleck on his own turf, I'll bet, Baxter had found himself speculating. A sedentary, indoor person, he surmised. Probably a salesman. Fortyish.

This man, Baxter had decided, did not interest him. It was the box and the promise of the 'fascinating documents' it might hold which intrigued him.

"The box," said Baxter continuing his narrative, "was approximately two and a half feet square, and old." Baxter went on to explain that its exterior was pine and pitted, the color a dull red, indicating that it had been treated long since with the red ocher which eighteenth and nineteenth century Maritimers so often used to protect their tool boxes and work tables.

Baxter said that he had been civil to his caller, but not friendly, because he hadn't liked the cut of the man's jib. Reluctantly, he had ushered the stranger into the study and told him to be quick about whatever business he had.

In keeping with Baxter's stipulation, the caller had wasted no time, apparently convinced that he was on insecure ground and borrowed time, that he would have to state his business quickly or be asked to leave.

Baxter said he had been surprised by his caller's apparent discomfiture - an unease he thought disproportionate to what did not seem a stressful situation and out of character for a man who had so aggressively thrust himself forward. But when Brooks, or whatever his name was, set the box down on the desk with such obvious relief, Baxter had concluded that the man had simply felt awkward holding it. That was until he observed that his visitor's hand shook when he inserted a key in the small lock.

But as soon as 'Brooks' had lifted the lid, Baxter said that he all but forgot about the man and his peculiarities. His attention was riveted on the box's interior. Just as Brooks had intimated, it appeared to be crammed full of old papers. Though these were much discolored by age, the writing on the top page - the only page visible - seemed legible.

Standing as he was some five feet away from his visitor and from the box, Baxter said that he had been unable to read any of the close-knit script, but immediately thought that it resembled his great-grandfather's hand - writing he was familiar with through entries in the family Bible. "Actually," Baxter said, turning first to me and then to Jim, "Great-grandfather's handwriting was quite unlike anyone else's. My mother said that, because of the extraordinary number of loops and the regularity of the letters, it looked as if it had been knitted. I figured," he went on, "that if I could just get a closer look I would be certain."

But just as he was about to step forward to take a closer look at the manuscript, Baxter continued, the stranger had let go of the lid. It had fallen back on its hinges, disclosing a meticulous carving which had caused Baxter to stop in his tracks and catch his breath in astonishment and excitement. There, inside the lid was a miniaturized *Angelina* inlaid in teak, butternut and ivory. The vessel's name was inscribed on its hull, his great-grandfather's initials carved in large letters in the pine beneath the inlaid vessel.

"I just couldn't believe it," Baxter said turning to Jim and me. "Still can't. Imagine! After all these years who'd ever think that such an amazing piece of the past would surface? I guess I was so taken aback that I just stood there staring for a couple of seconds. Any doubts I'd had about the man were, I suppose, allayed by what I interpreted as his act of good faith in bringing me such a treasure. At the back of my mind then I suppose I thought we were about to embark on a conversation about our relationship - which I now assumed this Brooks fellow could prove. But first I knew I had to have a closer look at the box. I started to step forward.

"Not so fast there," ordered my caller, now sounding neither hesitant nor eager to please.

"I looked up to find that he had a .38 aimed at my midriff."

-27-

Baxter's recital of the remaining events leading up to his beating and the vandalizing of his house was precise and so carefully articulated that his voice sounded like that of a person learning to speak again after throat surgery. Everything which had happened that night, he reiterated, had been so bizarre and unexpected that he admitted he felt reluctant to reflect on and recount the appalling facts. So it was with obvious effort that he took up where he had left off.

"As soon as my 'cousin' had me covered, he took a whistle from his shirt pocket and blew it sharply, twice I think - a signal, apparently. Right on cue, it seemed, two athletic-looking young fellows came bounding through the front door, slammed it shut and burst into the study. Tearing after them - not on cue - was Bruiser, teeth bared, hackles raised.

"On seeing Bruiser the men looked amazed and terrified - so totally nonplussed for a few seconds that, if I hadn't been so concerned about Bruiser's safety and my own, I might have laughed. But the tables weren't really turned. The two young thugs pulled knives and 'Cousin Brooks' turned his gun on the poor dog. If I hadn't spoken up to calm Bruiser, telling him to lie down, I expect he wouldn't be here now."

As he spoke, Baxter leaned over and patted Bruiser who thumped his tail in response but did not lift his head.

"I still find it hard to believe that this old boy broke out of the kitchen," Baxter continued reflectively, his left hand motionless on Bruiser's head. "When he heard the whistle and the men running, he must have charged that swinging door between the kitchen and dining room. As you know, I always leave Bruiser in the kitchen when I go out because he stays put there. I think I told you, Angela, that when Bruiser was a puppy someone came through that door when he was lying on the other side and he never forgot the bump he got. He's stayed clear of it since - until now."

I nodded, remembering.

Baxter was silent for so long that I thought he wasn't going to tell us any more that evening. Jim crossed and uncrossed his legs, a prelude, I thought, to suggesting a cup of tea or a nightcap before going home. But before Jim actually got up or said anything, Baxter began again.

Brooks, he told us, had sounded furious as soon as he had more or less recovered from Bruiser's surprise appearance. 'Put the damn dog down cellar,' he had shouted at Baxter. 'I'd shoot him if it wasn't for the noise.'

Jim whistled almost under his breath and Bruiser looked up. "So that explains how Bruiser was in the basement. I couldn't figure that out. I was pretty sure only you or Angela could have got him to go down those steps."

"Anyhow, to cut this recital short," Baxter resumed, "after I'd put Bruiser downstairs, Brooks told me that, as I'd suspected, he wasn't a cousin - long-lost or distant. On the other hand, he hadn't made everything up either. There was a connection, he told me. Our great-grandfathers' paths had crossed. You won't believe how. His great-grandfather lured mine onto the rocks, destroying the *Angelina III*."

Baxter paused and glanced over at me as if to let me know that he'd seen the newspaper clipping in his great-grandfather's log book that afternoon and partly grasped its significance - that such treachery was a hazard of the times up and down the Atlantic coast. I suspected too he wanted to assure me that he didn't intend just then to let Jim in on our secret about the cave and my findings there.

According to Brooks, his great-grandfather had been one of a substantial number of Maritimers who made their livings as 'wreckers' in the days of sailing ships. Apparently, sounding quite proud of his forebear, he'd told Baxter that the *Angelina III* had been among the scores of vessels his ancestor, presumably with the help of a gang he recruited, had caused to founder in fog or storms at various rocky coastal headlands not far from where legitimate lights were supposed to be. Sometimes, he'd said, warming to his subject, in a really bad blow one ship after another struck the rocks. After the seas subsided and the wrecks could be assessed, the men worked day and night salvaging whatever they figured was most saleable. Sometimes the profits were huge. The risks the wreckers took were usually minimal.

"It was a pretty neat scam," Brooks had smirked. "After all," he had continued, "who could tell for sure in those days how a ship went aground and broke up. No radar. No planes. No ship-to-shore communications.... And not too many survivors going around telling tales either. By the time the wrecked vessel was spotted - if it ever was - the wreckers had skedaddled. Not much risk at all. Too bad those old days are past."

"Brooks sounded genuinely regretful that he hadn't lived back then," Baxter remarked grimacing.

Neither Jim nor I spoke. We didn't want to distract Baxter from his recital of the events which had occurred that night.

*   *   *

Baxter went on then to voice the mounting fear he'd felt about why Brooks was telling him all this at gunpoint. As well, he couldn't help wondering how Brooks had learned about these long-ago doings.

Brooks had either guessed what Baxter was thinking or had been about to tell him anyway.

"I discovered all this about a year ago," Brooks dragged on. "I had these two" - he gestured to the two young men - "taking down the barn at the old place. It's still in our family," he had added. "Just like this old house is in yours.... Well, under the floorboards - you know how great they built back then, with double floors and all - between the studs they came across this box, an old ledger and some other stuff. Nothing that looked valuable, though, at a quick glance.

"I didn't even go through the papers till about a week later. When I got around to them I found stuff that made me think. I decided to dig into some of the possibilities. Now this is getting closer to where you come in."

By this time, Baxter told us, Brooks' sidekicks were growing increasingly restless. He guessed they weren't much for talking themselves, and they looked more and more resentful of their boss's long-windedness. "If Brooks hadn't kept waving that gun around, I think those two might have mutinied just about then," Baxter reflected.

"Anyway," Baxter went on, "Brooks wasn't finished yet. It was as if he'd never had a captive audience before." Baxter said he guessed that, under ordinary circumstances, Brooks' listeners walked away as soon as he launched into a long-winded explanation.

"Brooks went on to tell me," Baxter continued, "that his great-grandfather had kept an exact count of the vessels he and his cronies had wrecked. He had recorded their saleable contents, the prices the goods had fetched, even how much the men he'd employed earned from each wreck....

"His ledgers were just like a regular businessman's," Brooks had volunteered with obvious pride. "Great-granddaddy must have been one smart guy," he said. "Why, if he'd left his boys even a small fraction of what he took in, his whole family would've been rich. *I*'d have been rich. Maybe not as rich as old K.C., but rich enough. Then I wouldn't be here today," he'd babbled on waving his .38 in Baxter's face and leering unpleasantly, working himself up, Baxter had surmised, over the loss of those imagined ill-gotten millions several generations ago.

"Now this is where you really fit in," Brooks had said then, staring intently at Baxter and waving his gun as if to emphasize the point he was making. "That box there *was* your great-grandfather's - must've been on his boat, the *Angelina III*. Great-granddaddy must've wrecked her. There's nothing in it now except that top page," he said then, smirking and following Baxter's eyes to the box. "Only padding. That top page was a lure like the lights my Great-grandaddy lit for yours - to throw you off before my boys came in and I had my gun out."

"Meanwhile, all these analogies were really getting Brooks' sidekicks down," Baxter noted. "Gun or no gun, Brooks couldn't keep on much longer in this vein. But Brooks didn't seem to notice his cronies' restlessness: he rambled on.

"There was lots of letters and a map - well, part of a map of the Bay of Fundy. It was torn in half at a worn fold. On the piece I have an island is circled. You know, like a treasure map you imagine finding when you're a kid.

"Well, we found the island. I won't tell you where it is, but it was well worth discovering. We've put it to good use."

"Hey, don't tell him everything you know even if we're gonna get rid of him," the heftier of the two sidekicks had interjected angrily. "Let's get a move on...."

"Shut up," Brooks had snarled. "Can't you see I'm talking.... I'm almost done anyways.

"It wasn't the map that led me to you," Brooks went on. "Not even the box. It was something else in that box. An old letter. The first page of a letter to *your* great-grandaddy. I've read it over a bunch of times. I remember it all, highfalutin lingo that it is:

I know, my dear Captain, how carefully you will guard and stow away this precious document. You once told me you possessed a secret hiding place in your abode. Please store these papers in this safe place. When the time comes, the invaluable information contained therein will make us both rich men. We have only to bide our time.

"Now you, dear Cousin, live in the *Angelina*'s Captain's abode - *house* in normal language, right? And I've come to find out where that secret hiding place is. I figured that, when the *Angelina III* was wrecked, her captain died and maybe never got to tell his partner - or whoever wrote that letter - the location of the hiding place. It's hard to tell, though: the letter, I figure, was written about a year before the *Angelina III* went down."

After a significant pause, Baxter told us that Brooks had caught his breath and proceeded with his account. "I didn't have too much trouble tracking you down, *Cousin*. Llewellyn is not a common name in these here parts. And the local folks all want to help a stranger out. Just collar any old-timer around here and he'll spout off all he knows about you and your folks. We even heard you were going out tonight. That's why we picked this time to have a look-see on our own. Then if we weren't lucky - didn't find what we was after - we decided we'd stay on to welcome you home. But lucky us. Found you home. All set to help us out...."

Increasingly, Baxter said, the man sounded as if he was acting out the starring role in a film script he had written, produced and was directing. He seemed as interested in his own singular performance as in the outcome of his interview and Baxter said he felt sure that, if Brooks had gone on in the same way much longer, he could not control his henchmen. Spellbound by his own recital Brooks seemed to expect no response from his captive listener.

Baxter said he saw no point in interrupting Brooks' flood of words. He said he figured that as long as Brooks kept talking, he wasn't going to be assaulted.

Seeming oblivious to his sidekicks' increasing restlessness Brooks rambled on, gazing up at the packed bookshelves. "Maybe you already got the treasure. Maybe you or your dad - or his dad - tapped into the old bastard's cache and that's how you live like this."

Brooks, Baxter reported, had again gestured left and right with his right hand - the one holding the gun.

"This is a lot like the library in the Saint John museum archives where they helped me track you down - only better," Brooks had gone on spitefully. "I told them that I wanted to find out more about my family history - which was true," he had smirked, moving closer to Baxter. "In fact, I think I'm getting a taste for genealogical research - that's what the librarian called what I was doing -" he'd said confidentially, savoring the new word he'd added to his vocabulary. "You know they told me at the museum that nearly everyone gets hooked researching their family's history."

*   *   *

If it hadn't been for the two young men with the knives who looked increasingly as if they wanted to use them, Baxter told us, he might have tried to grab the gun from Brooks, who seemed so caught up in his story that he appeared almost to have forgotten about the weapon he was holding. He appeared, too, increasingly unable to separate past from present, fact from conjecture. Interrupting himself, he had suddenly asked Baxter point blank where the loot was, as if Baxter had been in touch with his great-grandfather recently.

It was, Baxter told us, only after he had disclaimed any knowledge of secret hiding places or caches of valuables that the men had almost immediately turned violent. Baxter said he had just begun an explanation about how, though it looked like a mansion, his house had probably not cost much more than $1,000 when it was built. He had remarked that lumber and labor were incredibly cheap then, that all his family had done since his great-grandfather's time was maintain the place.

Although Brooks had shown plenty of patience with his own long-drawn-out explanation, he had, Baxter said, demonstrated that he had a very short attention span when listening to Baxter - especially when it had become clear that no useful information would be forthcoming. Recognizing the shift in their boss's attitude, the two young thugs had quickly stepped forward and begun to work Baxter over.

"We'll get him to talk," he remembered hearing them say. He thought that they too sounded as if they'd seen too many violent movies and TV shows. Aping the lingo of such films, they said they'd use their knives to cut him up a little. That would be a preliminary, Baxter had guessed, to a more serious assault. Baxter said he recalled stepping back from the men and bumping into his desk chair. He must, he thought, have tripped or been hit then. He didn't remember. He speculated that the men had ransacked the house after he lost consciousness.

"I really don't remember anything more until I heard your voices," Baxter reflected. "Even then they sounded so far away that I wasn't sure whether they were real or imaginary. I don't remember how I got here.

"Oh, Jim, by the way," Baxter had added quickly, "you should know that one of the young fellows - the one I half recognized but couldn't place - had your knife, or one exactly like it. You know, the hand-wrought one with the mottled red and green handle that you thought you lost."

-28-

Jim ended up sleeping on the living room couch. When he left the next morning on a business trip to Saint John, Baxter and I decided we had better plan our next moves carefully. Staying put was out of the question.

We had told Jim not to expect to see either of us when he returned from Saint John, that we'd have to stay away from home until we could figure out what to do. "No," I told him before he asked, "we don't know where we're going" - adding that it would be just as well if he really had no idea of our whereabouts. Then suddenly remembering Vernon and Martha, I called out when he was already opening the door, "And don't forget to tell your folks we're not home, so they won't worry. Make up a reason. You can do that, can't you?"

"Ummm, OK," said Jim smiling as he wished us well and told us to take care.

Brooks was undoubtedly not through with Baxter. But before we decided what to do next, Baxter told me he had to fill me in on the facts he hadn't revealed the preceding evening. Most of these pertained to the cave.

He told me how he had discovered the cave by chance one time when Vernon had taken him, along with Jim, Lyle and Mac, to the island. He was, he said, eight or nine years old.

It had been a fine autumn day. While Vernon worked, the boys had played hide-and-seek, but, as usual, Baxter had been unable to keep up with the others. That was when he had tried to find a hiding place near at hand, one the others could not easily discover. He had needed, he said, to lie low for a bit, to recover in private without letting on to his buddies how ill he felt.

Looking around for a secluded place, he'd spotted the tangle of blackberry bushes, and, remembering the story of Peter Rabbit hiding out in a patch of brambles, he decided to hunker down in their midst if he could. He'd felt pretty sure, he said, that the others would never think of looking for him there.

Carefully, Baxter explained, he had worked his way into the midst of the blackberry patch. Though he had repeatedly snagged his clothes, he had persevered. Nevertheless, he had been almost ready to abandon this as a hiding place when he'd come upon the wooden trap door and lain down to rest on it. The door had been old and rickety. Since no one had lived on the island for twenty-five years or more, the door had not been repaired.

As he lay there, face down on the warm, dry boards, the boy had begun to wonder why the door was there. Perhaps, he thought, the boards might conceal a well. He'd pushed a stone through a crack just under his nose, but there had been no splash. He'd then squirmed forward to look through a larger crack where some of the wood had disintegrated - and that was when the middle part of the old door had given way and he had fallen onto the dirt floor beneath.

Lying there shaken and bruised at the bottom of what seemed to be a hole, he had called for help again and again. When no one came to his rescue after what had seemed like hours, he'd gotten up and begun feeling his way around his prison. He had found steps leading up out of the root cellar, but he hadn't been strong enough to push the door up. And, since the hole he'd fallen through was not near the steps, he hadn't been able to get out.

So, Baxter explained, he had crawled back down again and felt around for something - a box maybe - that he could push beneath the opening and climb up on. He had found the root cellar shelves, but they were attached to the wall in the passageway. He came upon the old jars too, but found nothing to suit his purpose.

When he had reached the back of the passageway, still feeling his way, he had discovered the looped rope. Giving it a tug, he had seen the cave suddenly disclosed, sunlight pouring down into it from the apertures above. He had thought then that he was safe - that the light meant that he could get out through the cave.

So he had entered the large chamber and seen that the light all appeared to come from the ceiling high above his head. He had exchanged one prison for another, he thought, and he had begun to cry. Through his tears, he took in details of the cave and realized it must once have been used as quite an elaborate hideaway - elaborate because someone had taken the trouble to embed a number of iron rings in the granite. Ropes, and in one instance a chain, had been looped through these rings, though the rope had long since disintegrated. Only fragments of hemp had remained on the floor.

The chain, the boy noticed, descended from the wall into what appeared to be a large, dark rectangular pit. Going to the edge of this opening and peering down, the boy had seen what appeared to be another cave. A worn stone staircase led down into it.

Baxter described how he had gone down the steps and found himself, as he had expected, in another cave. Not far from the base of the stone staircase was an opening onto the shale beach. He had walked out into the sunlight and made his way back along the beach to where the others were still playing hide-and-seek.

Baxter hadn't told them what had happened. In fact, he said he had never told anyone until now.

Later, when Vernon and the boys had boarded the fishing boat and chugged out of the protected cove on their homeward way, Baxter said he'd looked back towards the beach, expecting to see the cave entrance. But the tide had come in: beach and cave had vanished. To the small boy, it seemed almost as if his private adventure had never taken place. He was eager to forget it too when he had suddenly realized what would have happened to him if he had gone down into the lower cave at the wrong time. Just the thought of being trapped by the tide made him squirm. He had decided to pretend - even to himself - that nothing had occurred. And until a year ago, Baxter told me smiling ruefully, he had never had any desire to go back to the island.

Then, last summer, he said, when he'd been sailing the *Black Angel* with Mac in the vicinity of Sheep Island, he had, on the spur of the moment, wanted to land. He'd felt he had to revisit the cave.

As luck would have it, the tide was right and Mac agreeable to putting in. Mac had said he'd fish off the rocks while Baxter had a look around.

Baxter hadn't told Mac then what he had in mind. He'd just headed off to the bramble patch and located the wooden door without much difficulty. Once there, what had surprised him was that the door had been repaired - with weathered boards, it was true, but sound ones nonetheless.

Anyway, Baxter went on to explain how he'd lifted the door and gone through the same rigmarole as he had so many years earlier. But everything in the cave's interior was different. He had found a Zodiac on a platform and the cave full of boxes, just as I had. He had also discovered another cave - an even larger one - which opened up behind the main one. He reckoned I hadn't seen it because the piled boxes hid the entrance. He said he hadn't found out what was in the adjoining cave. It was dark, without the 'skylights' of the main cave, and he had had no flashlight.

"And of course I didn't find the wall safe," Baxter interjected at this point. Obviously, until you spotted it, no one's come upon that since my great-grandfather - or someone else - put the logs, the diary and the other papers in it."

Because the platform on which the Zodiac rested had covered the stone steps which led down to the lower cave, and because the tide was still too far in, Baxter said he'd left the way he had entered.

He had intended to take Mac into his confidence. No one, he reminded me, is more tight-lipped than Mac. Together, Baxter decided, they would enter the caves from the shore when the tide had retreated sufficiently.

But Baxter said he never did tell Mac because, when he got back to where Mac was fishing, Mac had his own story to relate. He had said that, while Baxter had been off exploring, two strangers in a large and powerful pleasure craft had hovered at the entrance to the cove - almost as if they planned to enter it as soon as the tide was fully in again.

Mac said he'd waved but they hadn't reponded. He had told Baxter that he was pretty sure he had never seen the man at the wheel, but that the young fellow in the stern looked familiar. His silhouette, the way he moved when he shifted boxes from one pile to another, struck a chord somewhere far back in his consciousness. He just couldn't remember exactly why. Maybe, he explained, the young fellow was a fisherman's helper. He had certainly moved, Mac said, as if he was used to boats. Perhaps, he speculated, he was from away and he had briefly encountered him on the wharf in fishing season.

-29-

Within two hours of Jim's departure, Baxter and I had left the house. Having finally finished putting our stories together and considered their combined impact, the conclusions we came to were, inevitably, terrifying. By staying put we were undoubtedly easy targets for men who would probably stop at nothing. The more we thought about the vulnerability of our position, the more surprising it seemed that we had escaped an attack during the days of Baxter's recovery.

Despite our danger, I could understand why Baxter had opposed calling in the police. Given all the circumstances, his wanting to have a crack at solving the multiple mysteries involving his attackers made sense to me. I just couldn't see how he thought he could do it.

What was driving him was not, I realized, a sudden recognition of his calling as a criminal investigator, but an overwhelming reluctance to hand over his great-grandfather's papers to anyone. An equally important motivation in his decision to play the sleuth was his fear that, once word leaked out that a cache of valuables from the old days - or at least clues to its whereabouts - might be secreted in his house, other treasure-seekers and the media too would almost certainly descend upon him, destroying his privacy and generally making his life miserable.

It was also horribly apparent to me - and presumably to Baxter as well - that, if we didn't get to the bottom of this business quickly, Brooks and his buddies would be back to deal not only with Baxter but with Jim and me as well. When Brooks found out that we were Baxter's rescuers, he would assume that both of us were his confidants too. And when Brooks learned that the police had not been informed of his visit to Baxter's house, he probably wouldn't hesitate to act.

One advantage we could count on, Baxter noted, giving the words his old ironical twist, was the fact that Brooks and his boys weren't going to publicize what they knew. If we were able to keep out of their way for a few days, while investigating on our own, we just might be able to sort things out, he reasoned. But if we didn't succeed in short order, he reminded me, then we'd have to go to the police to save our skins. He emphasized the *we* and *our*. Sink or swim we were in this together. And, despite the dangerous nature of this bond, I found that I was considerably moved and surprisingly pleased by this enforced close partnership with Baxter.

Meanwhile, Baxter's biggest worry - and mine - was that Brooks and company might have guessed that one or both of us had found the cave and seen the contraband it contained. Obviously they knew about my trips to the island with the sheep. As well, they had seen Mac's fishing boat anchored off the cove and perhaps even spotted Baxter on the shale beach below the caves. What if, despite my care, I had left some telltale sign behind after my sojourn in the cave during the storm? And suppose one of the men had noticed that the kerosene levels in the wall niche lamp or the heater were down?

If they suspected we knew about their hideaway and the illicit goods secreted there, getting rid of us quickly and permanently would be their probable decision. Brooks would hardly hang around indefinitely in hopes of turning up clues to a more than a century-old treasure which might no longer be traceable - might, if you came right down to it, never have existed. Even if he was prepared to wait a while, his impatient sidekicks probably would not. I concluded from Baxter's observations about their temperaments that, if Brooks wanted to put on the brakes, they would almost certainly mutiny.

*   *   *

I should have guessed that Baxter's fertile mind wouldn't rest until it formulated a plan to extricate us from this mess. Actually, his scheme turned out to be a counter attack rather than an escape. It involved a series of daring moves I never would have thought of - certainly would not have attempted on my own.

My introduction to our joint participation in Baxter's plan began with one of Baxter's typically low-keyed statements - low-keyed because of his deadpan delivery: "Come on, Angela, we've got to get out of here before we get any older: otherwise, we won't be getting older."

Despite the seriousness of our situation and its ugly possibilities, which Baxter had half humorously touched on, I couldn't help smiling as I asked him what he had in mind. He shut me up by saying that there wasn't time to talk any more, that if we hung around discussing our situation, we'd be sitting ducks.... "To coin a phrase!" he laughed, mocking his own use of a cliché.

So when Baxter said peremptorily, "Follow me," and set off towards the shore on foot at a surprisingly fast pace - fast, considering his recent injuries - I did indeed hurry after him.

While we had been discussing our situation earlier, Baxter had said that he wanted to go back to his property, to the boathouse. Going by car as far as his house was obviously out of the question, so I found no difficulty agreeing with the direction he was taking when I imagined the alternative - the possibility of being ambushed somewhere along his sylvan driveway or near the house itself.

How, I asked myself, could Jim have been so foolhardy as to return to the house to investigate and clean up? At the time, I reminded myself, I had agreed to his going. We must have been out of our minds.

Since Baxter was still probably not up to the long trudge through the woods from our place to his, the only reasonable way to reach his boathouse did seem to be by water. And so we putt-putted our way close in along the shore in my twelve foot aluminum dingy with the 7½ h.p. motor. Even then, I cut the motor before rounding the point and rowed into the cove beneath the bluff, praying that Baxter's 'cousin' and his 'associates' were not lurking there. At least, I told myself, we'd have some warning if they were. Inkerman and Bruiser, and perhaps Jen too, could be counted on to let us know. Though the dinghy rode low in the water because of the Labs' extra weight, I didn't for a moment regret bringing them - or Jen either, for that matter, though her weight was negligible. Anyway, since we had no idea how long we'd be absent, we had no other choice.

I wished that Mac was with us. His strength, hardiness and calmness would, I reasoned, have helped sustain us. But when Baxter had called Mac's house - and I didn't know then what he had in mind - there had been no answer.

I fretted when I began to realize what was in store for us. Baxter was not really strong enough for a venture such as we were about to undertake - even at the best of times. Without his having the physical reserves that our present position was likely to call for, our situation seemed especially precarious. I wished I knew how to handle the *Black Angel*. My ignorance in that department could hardly be remedied overnight. Sailing such a schooner had little in common with manoeuvering the *Bay Lady*.

*   *   *

Despite our qualms, the dogs gave no sign that strangers might be in the vicinity of the boathouse. Jumping out of the dinghy as soon as we touched the beach, they sniffed around and explored with their usual interest and thoroughness without seeming to discover anything worth getting excited about. Their reconnaissance completed, they galloped back to us as if to let us know that they considered this the most enjoyable of outings. And, when Baxter went to open the boathouse doors, we found no one lurking nearby - no sign, either, of anyone having tampered with the locks.

With any luck, I told myself, Brooks' 'researches' hadn't extended to the *Black Angel*. Perhaps no one had mentioned her.

Launching the *Black Angel* and getting her under way had been easier than I could ever have imagined. Baxter's natural fastidiousness, together with his fixation on the schooner, had ensured that she was always ready to sail. The pulleys had worked as well as Baxter had predicted. Better even. The tide was high, and we were blessed with fine weather - a clear day with a steady breeze.

"Just the day for a fair weather sailor like me," Baxter had quipped. And from the slight catch in his voice, I guessed he was excited, even looking forward to taking the *Black Angel* out of mothballs.

Baxter, invariably one to hide his light under a bushel, as my grandmother would have said, demonstrated a surprising reserve of strength. Although he was long and lean to the point of excessive thinness, he appeared to have no difficulty raising the mainsail with only minimal help from me.

I had to admire the way he moved about the vessel. He was attuned to everything about that schooner. Anticipating her every motion, he handled her so well single-handedly that he made manoeuvering her look easy. Although I hovered nearby, he didn't really need my help. It was clear that his knowledge of sailing was by no means just theoretical. I was impressed - and relieved.

We skimmed over the water with what seemed to me as much grace and ease as the gulls and terns which flew in our wake. After several uneventful hours we had crossed the bay, anchored, clambered into our dingy and tied it up at the government wharf below Mac's brother's house. While Baxter was endeavoring to point the house out to me, Mac materialized on the wharf above us.

Typically, he didn't say anything, just stood there, rocklike - a formidable presence, waiting for us to notice him. The relief and joy we felt on seeing him must have been obvious, for Mac, who rarely smiled, began to grin broadly. He appeared to be as happy to see us as we him - that was until we filled him in with a few of the pertinent details about the danger we were in and the help we wanted him to give us.

-30-

We spent the rest of the day and that night at Mac's brother's place, a rambling, somewhat dilapidated farmhouse with fields and woods stretching down to the bay. From my bedroom window I could see the wharf and Mac's fishing boat tied up alongside five or six others. Mac's brother's wife, Janet, pointed one out as belonging to her husband, George. Offshore in deeper water, the *Black Angel* rode at anchor, an aristocratic anachronism - an expensive model privateer.

George and Janet are probably fortyish, a good ten to twelve years older than Mac, Baxter and I. Janet told me that their three children - a girl and two boys - are nine, eleven and twelve. She's very wrapped up in them - and her garden, which she was eager to show me, although, as she said, there weren't a lot of things up. "You'll have to get Mac and Baxter to bring you back at the end of the summer," she said, glowing with enthusiasm. "Things look great then."

It was because of the extended tour of the property which Janet and Sharon, her nine-year-old, took me on that I missed hearing about the plans Mac and Baxter had hatched for the next day and putting in my two cents' worth.

The plus side of this foray was that neither Janet nor I had to make supper. George, Baxter and Mac had prepared burgers and condiments while we were on our mini-excursion.

Baxter told me at supper that we'd better get a good night's sleep because we were going to leave at dawn. This time of year that meant about five. We'd have to be up and breakfasting shortly after four, Baxter had said pointedly. He offered to call me so that I wouldn't sleep in.

As it turned out, it was Baxter who needed the call. Janet, the children and I had gone to bed soon after the supper dishes were done and the table set for breakfast. Baxter, Mac and George were still going strong when we'd said good night. Beers in hand, they looked as if they'd settled in for a companionable evening. I fell asleep listening to the murmur of their voices and their laughter as they swapped stories.

I had wanted to ask what Baxter meant by *we*. Was it to be just Baxter and me, or was Mac going along? And what about George? How much, I wondered, had Baxter told the brothers about what had happened? And above all, why hadn't he told me where we were going and which boat we were taking? One of the fishing boats, I presumed. I was put out with Baxter for keeping these things from me. We were partners after all; in this together, deeper than the others.

-31-

By dawn we were under way as planned, but in the *Black Angel*, *not* Mac's fishing boat. *We* turned out to be Mac, Baxter and me. George was still in bed, Janet told us when she served breakfast and made our picnic lunch.

The dogs had not moved from the pads Janet had allotted them in the mud room. She and the children, she said, were going to enjoy dog-sitting while we were gone.

The day was as clear as the preceding one, the breeze somewhat stronger, but still steady. It seemed to me that we were hung with horseshoes to have two such days in succession just when we needed them. I was surprised that there was no sign of the early morning fog so generally prevalent on Passamaquoddy Bay at this time of year: no indication either that the weatherman's gale force winds - prophesied for later in the day - would occur.

Almost immediately after our departure, Baxter came aft to talk to me. He apologized for not telling me earlier what was going on, but explained that he hadn't wanted to let on to George and Janet that our sail across the bay was anything more than a pleasure trip. He told me he'd had to explain to Mac about the trouble we were in, quickly, while George wheeled out the barbecue and made brief forays into the house for food. He said he'd told Mac about the attack, the cave and its contents, including the 'wall safe' repository of his great-grandfather's papers.

"I didn't see how I could ask for Mac's help without explaining what we were up against," Baxter said earnestly, watching my face carefully to see how I reacted. "If anyone in this world is trustworthy and able to keep a secret, it's Mac," Baxter hurried on when I didn't offer any opinion. "I'd trust him with my life." He paused and laughed, still watching my expression, then added; "but I guess that's what we're doing, isn't it?"

"Who knows?" I replied. "You still haven't mentioned where we're going." If I sounded miffed, I was.

"Now for the plan...." Baxter continued, appearing oblivious to my censorious tone. "We're on our way to the island, and if the coast seems clear when we get there, you and I are going back to the cave to get the rest of the papers from the 'wall safe'. Anything we can't take with us we'll photograph. Mac will stand guard on the *Black Angel*. He's to fire a cannon as a warning if 'our friends' show up. A cannon is probably the only signal we could hear.

"What do you think? Are you game?"

To say that I was taken aback by Baxter's plan is putting it mildly. I'd hoped we were going to get out of harm's way for the next few days, plan our strategies in safety and at our leisure. I thought too that we'd give Baxter more time to recover - though I had to admit he looked better than usual, which was hard to understand. It seemed to me that we were on our way to participate in the most dangerous scenario anyone could dream up, given the circumstances. To top it all off, our warning if we were in danger of being trapped was to be the boom of an early nineteenth century cannon.

"You can't be serious," I said for lack of a more original protest.

"I'm not surprised you didn't tell me last night what you had in mind. I'd have had horrible nightmares - or I wouldn't have slept at all.... Perhaps I wouldn't even have come along today at all," I added for good measure, still put out by what I considered to be Baxter's high-handedness.

"Playing games with dangerous criminals, using antiquated equipment too, isn't my idea of fun - even if it is yours and Mac's. For starters," I went on, "I can't see why you chose the *Black Angel* instead of Mac's fishing boat. You can't take her into the cove and leave her while we're in the cave. She'll be lying on her side as soon as the tide goes out, and we'll really be trapped. Probably, if I'd known what you had in mind, I wouldn't have come along today," I reiterated. "Your *plan* sounds as if it had been concocted by a couple of adventurous twelve year olds. I..."

Baxter laughed, interrupting. "But we're not going into the cove. We'll anchor off the rocks outside and use the dinghy to get to the nearest point. We won't be able to stay till the turn of the tide, but we should have more than an hour to get what we need from the cave. This way," he went on, "we shouldn't be interrupted. If our friends are planning on going to the island, they'll likely wait till the change of the tide.

"It's dangerous, I agree," Baxter continued, reading aright the skepticism in my eyes, "but you know what the old-time mariners used to say: if you're caught in a hurricane, head for its eye, and ride out the storm there. In a manner of speaking, that's what we're planning to do. Isn't that O.K. with you?"

"Not really," I said, sounding disagreeable even to my own ears. "I think we should hang around out here for the rest of the day. Tack back and forth, you know, in case Brooks and company are already on the island.... So we don't have any nasty surprises.... Provided it's true they don't know about the *Black Angel*, they'll have no reason to suspect that we're not simply rich visitors pleasure cruising.

"Just try to imagine Brooks and one of his henchmen holed up in that cave, ready to welcome us. At least let's wait and see if the Zodiac comes out on the falling tide," I pleaded.

Now Baxter was the one to look put out. "If we do that, chances are they'll bring their big boat in on the tide. They won't expect us now. We've got the element of surprise in our favor.

"Besides, I've got this," he said drawing out an archaic-looking gun, "just in case there is a confrontation."

I felt like asking him if he'd remembered his cutlasses. Baxter was sounding more and more as if he'd just stepped out of a Robert Louis Stevenson novel. But all I said was, "Another nineteenth century piece?" And then I couldn't help adding, "It really should be in a museum."

Truth to tell, I was disappointed in Baxter, though my disappointment also made me realize how greatly I'd valued him all along. I was frustrated with myself too. I hadn't wanted to quarrel with Baxter - to feel so antagonistic about a proposal he'd made. I felt sad, realizing more than ever how much his friendship meant to me, wanting to patch up our disagreement. I decided to hold my tongue for the time being.

But I couldn't help worrying about the way Baxter was so caught up in replaying the past, with all its attendant props - the schooner, the retractable cannons and now the antique gun.

-32-

Despite my concerns, everything seemed to go according to plan. Baxter and I got ashore easily in the dinghy. We hauled it up beyond reach of the waves and secured it to the corroded metal ring which Mac had told us about when we were half-way across the bay. He said he had come upon the ring the previous summer when he'd been waiting for Baxter to return from his visit to the cave, though of course, as he noted, he hadn't known about the cave then.

Mac said he figured the ring had been there a long time, and he admitted to being surprised that it was still so firmly embedded in the rock.

When I saw for myself how worn and corroded the ring was, I couldn't help wishing I knew something about whoever had put it there in the first place. This was, I thought to myself, just another instance of the merging of past and present which had marked this entire venture from the beginning, making it so unusual and, I had to admit, intriguing. Certainly, finding the contents of the cave's 'wall safe' had brought one old-timer, Baxter's great-grandfather, into a less blurred focus.

*   *   *

So it happened that, as we approached the blackberry patch, lifted up the old-new door and climbed down into the passageway leading to the cave, I found that my mind was more on the past than the present. I had shoved my doubts to the back of my mind and subscribed to Baxter's plan. After all, I reminded myself, Baxter was anything but foolhardy. No Robert Louis Stevenson or Dick Francis protagonist either.

Since Baxter had fallen silent as soon as we'd left the *Black Angel*, my preoccupation with things past had become increasingly intense, the present fading into obscurity. I was, as Baxter would have said if he hadn't been so wrapped up in his own thoughts, in a brown study.

Because of this mind set, I wasn't really afraid anymore, just tremendously keyed up and determined to do my best in recording the holdings in the wall safe. I promised myself that Baxter and I would spend tomorrow, after we got the films developed, poring over the words from the past. I was so excited by the prospect that I could scarcely breathe.

That was why, despite my original apprehensions, I was totally unprepared for what happened when I pulled the rope cord and the cave portal swung back. The cave was occupied. Baxter, no less shocked, it seemed, than I, obviously recognized the single occupant, a man whom I had never seen before. I guessed though, from Baxter's reaction that this was 'Cousin Brooks'.

-33-

The surprise was ours, not his. Brooks was, in fact, all set to receive us. Smirking, he sat in one of the chairs alongside the table with a gun - the .38, I supposed - pointed at us.

"Come on down," he beckoned. "Glad to see you. Been expecting you since Gordy radioed he'd seen you arrive on some fancy sailboat.... Eh, Gordy?" he said, apparently directing this observation to someone behind us and pretending cordiality. I could see what Baxter had meant about Brooks' staginess.

Gordy promptly identified himself by prodding me in the back. I stumbled forward down the stone steps alongside Baxter who must have received similar encouragement to descend promptly.

"So it *was* you folks who was in here before," Brooks continued conversationally, obviously enjoying himself now that he had us trapped and apparently just where he wanted us. Gordy here don't miss a trick," he said brandishing his weapon. "Don't know what I'd do without him. Got his training with a street gang in Noo York Cidy. Up till now he's been sort of bored 'round here. Had to lay low. This here's just up his alley. Keep him out of trouble." He laughed loudly at his own wit, and in spite of our predicament I thought of Gram's home-spun quip that 'the loud laugh speaks the vacant mind' - and then realized its seeming inaccuracy in the present situation. It seemed that Brooks' mind had not been at all vacant. Unfortunately.

"Ya, Gordy told me someone'd been here. Noticed the kerosene was way down when he went to light the heater. Same with that lamp. Some smart, eh?"

Gordy's response was a grunt, followed by a mumbled: "You talk too goddamn much. How 'bout some action?"

"Tie 'em up," Brooks said. "One to each of them extra rings.... And to think just last week we was wondering what their use was.... Too close to the ground, you said. Eh, Gordy? Now with these two settin' side by side on the floor it's picture perfect. What do you think now?"

But Brooks clearly didn't expect an answer.

Gordy tied us up quickly and efficiently while Brooks babbled and kept us covered. Brooks' patter, probably calculated to exasperate us, seemed to get on Gordy's nerves more than Baxter's and mine. Brooks' verbal needling was the least of our worries.

The rope Gordy used to tie us up was new nylon cord. Almost at once it began chafing my wrists, even with a minimum of squirming. I noticed that Baxter was miserable for the same reason. And after a few minutes I began to feel as if my shoulders were being dislocated by having my wrists so tightly bound behind my back.

It occurred to me that this was my first experience with torture and because of this I began to wonder, despite our discomfort and danger, how medieval prisoners, heretics and others, had borne torments like the rack and thumbscrews without recanting right away or divulging any information their torturers demanded. Funny, until I'd had this taste of misery myself - though admittedly not on the same scale - I'd never speculated about such things. Before now they hadn't seemed exactly believable.

Brooks looked incredibly pleased with himself. Having us in his power in a situation which promised to assure our cooperation was clearly much better luck than he had expected. Even Gordy had lightened up a little - though not for long, because he and Brooks soon began to argue about how they would proceed.

Before their argument became really heated, Baxter interrupted with a proposal which momentarily silenced Brooks and Gordy and left me stunned.

"O.K. Cousin," Baxter said in a decisive, take-charge kind of voice. "I give up. You win.... I'll tell you what you want to know.... The hiding place where great-grandfather's papers are.... Just let Angela and me go - expecially Angela. She doesn't have a clue about all this."

I tried to catch Baxter's attention, wanting to deter him from telling the men about the wall safe - right then anyway - but he wouldn't look at me. "Don't," I said finally, unable to contain myself.

That was when Gordy pulled his knife out of its handy belt case and held it close to my throat. "Wha'd you say?" he snarled. "You shut-up or I'll drop you down the hole under that there Zodiac." He jerked his head in the direction of the boat on the platform. "And when they find you - *if* they find you - all mashed to a pulp, they'll blame the tides and rocks in this hell hole of a bay. You understand? And I'm not like this goddam wimp I'm teamed up with just now. Dumpin' you wouldn't give me no nightmares. I sleep like a baby, no matter what."

I nodded, too terrified to speak. Baxter was right to give in, I thought. He could see the writing on the wall, as Gram would have said.

And when Gordy turned away to attend to Baxter and I pulled myself together somewhat, I was amazed that I had elicited such a wordy response from a man I'd thought could scarcely put a sentence together. Just another example, I thought, that no one was so easy to categorize as you believed when you first met them.... Or maybe it was just that Brooks' verbosity was catching.

"O.K. now let's have it," Gordy said to Baxter.

"How about untying us first, *Cousin*?" Baxter said to Brooks.

"Are you kiddin'? No way," Brooks replied promptly. "Not till we've got them papers."

"They're in my house," Baxter said, "in a special hiding place."

I gasped. So he wasn't going to tell them after all. But now, after the scare Gordy had given me, I didn't feel like witnessing any heroics.

"How about taking us there?" Baxter said. "Then I can show you."

"No way," Brooks repeated, more emphatically this time. "If yer lyin' we've got you here where you can't get away. Got you here till we get the truth."

Baxter was briefly silent. Then he began to explain slowly, thoughtfully, so slowly and thoughtfully that it seemed obvious to me he was making it up as he went along. It was hard to gauge what Brooks and Gordy thought.

"You remember that night you turned up at my place? You came in by the front door - into the big hall? Well, do you remember the steps leading upstairs from there?" Baxter didn't wait for an answer and Brooks and Gordy just nodded.

"Now listen carefully," Baxter went on intently. "The fourth step from the bottom is different from the others. Doesn't look it, but it is. It opens up so that there's a box-like hiding place. That's where great-grandfather's papers are."

How could they be? I reflected, knowing perfectly well that we'd taken the papers with us in the boat and that the rest were right above us in the wall safe. Baxter's going to get us killed when they find out he's not telling the truth, I speculated, thinking about the cave under the Zodiac and our bodies being swished around in the roiling tidewater and ground against the rocks.

"No.... No.... No.... The papers are not there," I wanted to scream. But I was too afraid to open my mouth. If I said anything at all, I thought, Gordy could well fulfil his threat. I'd had the impression that doing me in as he'd described wouldn't displease him, would maybe even relieve some of the tension he showed. I tuned in again to Baxter giving directions.

"The lip of each step juts out a little - about half an inch from the perpendicular board which holds it up. Feel around under this, on the left hand side. There's a tiny indentation. The wood there feels different from the rest. Press it. Then just lift the top of the step. It's hinged on the back and opens like a lid. Inside this box are the papers.... Oh, and if you don't believe they're great-grandfather's just compare the writing with the sample you've got, *Cousin*."

I had to admit that Baxter sounded increasingly convincing. If I hadn't known better, I'd probably have believed him myself. In spite of our precarious situation, I was impressed with his powers of invention.

Brooks and even Gordy looked as if they believed him.

Knowing all I knew, I found myself admitting privately just then that Baxter was turning out to be a disappointment: it wouldn't take Brooks and Gordy long to find out that Baxter was making all this up. Then they'd really turn on us. Baxter should have known better.

I suppose, because I'd held Baxter in high esteem for so long, I'd romanticized his capabilities. I'd imagined that if he was ever in a tight situation like this one he'd think of a subtle solution, an ingenious way out ... that he'd turn out to be something of a contemporary Scarlet Pimpernel. Instead, here he was weaving foolish tales that were bound to do us in.

Distressed about seeing Baxter suddenly in this new and unflattering light and sick about our dreadful predicament, I tuned out of most of what was going on around me. Everything seemed hopeless. I felt nauseous and light-headed. My attention became focused on not throwing up.

*   *   *

I was brought back to what was happening around me by the

violence of an argument which erupted suddenly between Brooks and Gordy.

"Goddam you son-of-a-bitch. You're not gonna leave me behind while you go off on this fuckin' wild goose chase after your wimpy pretend *cousin*'s granddaddy's papers. And just supposin' this pathetic jerk here *is* on the level, and you *do* find what we're after, what's to bring you back here to pick me up?

"These two don't need no guard. How do you think they're gonna get away? Just tell me that?"

Brooks didn't say anything, which I supposed meant that he was going to take Gordy along and leave us in the cave. I was beginning to feel hopeful. Once they left, and Mac saw them go - if only he was not too absorbed in tinkering with the motor - he'd wonder what was up and try to find us. I speculated that he might have some problems finding the cave, but at low tide and with the detailed account Baxter had given him, I hoped he'd succeed.

Gordy was busy with the pulleys and was apparently about to lower the platform and Zodiac when Brooks stopped him suddenly with a question.

"Hey, Gordy," he said, sounding stressed. "What about that fancy sailboat you said you saw out there? Don't you think these two would of left someone aboard? If it's as big as you said, maybe there's a whole crew - guys who'll come looking when *Cousin* and *Sheep Girl* here don't turn up."

"I thought about that already," Gordy replied. "Remember, I watched with binoculars when they came in. Didn't see no one else. If there'd been another guy, don't you think he'd a been up on deck lowering sails and helping these two into the dinghy?

"Anyhow, just s'pposin' another guy's on there. How's he gonna get ashore with the dinghy tied to the rocks? Swim, for crissake, in this water? Ice cakes was floatin' everywhere till a few weeks ago. Or did you ferget about that? This is the friggin' Bay of Fundy. Even in August the water's cold enough to finish anyone off right smart."

"S'ppose you're right," Brooks said. "But let's take a look see when we get outta here. Just to make sure."

"All this talk, you goddam fool," Gordy said. "Shut up, or we'll miss the fuckin' tide. Then we'll be trapped here till tomorrow night. Remember, Johnny won't be bringin' the *Ora* in till then."

Brooks, brought back to this reality, said no more. He jumped into the Zodiac with surprising agility, considering his unathletic build, and waited for Gordy to lower the platform. Gordy, no slouch when it came to action, climbed aboard and lowered away.

There must have been enough water to float the Zodiac because we heard the motor start and hum off into the distance. Relieved of its burden, the platform returned to its original position, blocking the hole to the lower cave.

-34-

"Yes, time and tide wait for no man," Baxter said with a grin when we could no longer hear the motor. He sounded so cheery that I was furious. Still nauseous as well. How could he be - or pretend to be - so upbeat when our situation was as serious as ever? Maybe worse. Didn't he realize that Brooks and Gordy might try to board the *Black Angel*?... Would then discover Mac and the papers? Would realize that Baxter had been lying...? Didn't he understand that if Mac was taken prisoner too there was no hope at all of our being rescued?

I couldn't believe that Baxter could be so obtuse. How could I have thought that he was more perceptive than any other man I'd known? I could only conclude that that knockout blow had addled his brains.

Because I was so distressed, I gave Baxter a modified version of what was going through my mind. He didn't seem one bit chastened.

"Angela, pin your hopes on Mac. You won't be disappointed. I realize you don't know him very well. But he's more than a match for those two. Yes, even Gordy," he said, reading my mind.

"They'll never catch him off guard. Mac doesn't say much, but he doesn't miss a thing either. He'll hear their motor and see the Zodiac.

"And how do you imagine they could get aboard the *Black Angel* without his help? Besides, I'd bet anything Gordy won't let Brooks get too close to her. He'd see right off how vulnerable they'd be."

"Well, perhaps so," I allowed. "But I still can't see what you're so cheery about. We're trussed up like a couple of turkeys about to be roasted and you seem as pleased as if you'd just won the lottery. Brooks and Gordy are gone, but they'll be back in a couple of hours. Then what?"

Baxter laughed out loud. "What a worrywart you are, Angela! First of all, I should let you know that that stair box actually exists - and it really is full of great-grandfather's papers."

I was too surprised to speak, so Baxter proceeded with his explanation.

"What it will take Brooks and Gordy some time to discover is that these aren't the papers they are looking for. It would take Brooks days to decipher that handwriting. Remember the knitted look it has?"

"But...," I interrupted.

"Now, I'm not too pleased with the possibility of losing these family papers either, and I had planned to go back over them in light of your recent find here in the cave. Still, I thought that, given the situation we're in, sacrificing them might be in order... especially since I have a photocopy in the bank's safe deposit box."

"Well," I admitted, somewhat mollified, "that's better than I hoped. But, once they think they've got the papers, they'll still be back to deal with us.... And I can't imagine why they'd want to keep us around. If they dropped us down the hole when the tide's in, they wouldn't run much risk of getting charged for murder. And Gordy sounded as if he'd really enjoy getting rid of us like that. He's apparently got no compunction about doing someone in." I shuddered, suddenly chilled to the bone.

"I'm counting on Mac finding us," Baxter said. "When he hears and sees that Zodiac he's going to wonder if we've met up with those two and he'll come looking for us. With any luck, after the description I gave him of the cave, he'll find us."

"You forget," I chipped in crossly, "that he can't get off the *Black Angel*. As Gordy pointed out just before he and Brooks took off, the dinghy's tied up on the point."

"Well, getting ashore should be no problem for Mac," Baxter replied agreeably. There is another inflatable raft - sort of a mini-Zodiac - stowed on the *Black Angel*. Mac knows where it is. He helped me stow it. Don't forget..."

An explosion interrupted Baxter's explanation.

"They've blown up the *Black Angel*," I whispered. "Blown Mac up too."

I looked sideways at Baxter, but he still seemed unperturbed. "I hardly think so, Angela. When they lowered the Zodiac we'd have seen if they had explosives with them. There was nothing in the Zodiac. Remember? And they aired no plans for blowing anything up. An undertaking like that would take some organizing.

"No, I'll bet Brooks and Gordy are halfway across the bay. That booming sound was one of the *Black Angel*'s cannons - our agreed-on warning shot. Now Mac'll be waiting for us to turn up. And when we don't, he'll come looking. Hide-and-seek, with the seeker well provided with clues!"

-35-

Baxter was right. Mac didn't take long coming to our rescue. Typical fisherman though, he'd decided to explore the possibilities closest to the sea rather than walk inland even as far as the root cellar entrance. So we heard him in the cave beneath us hallooing and shouting our names. His voice sounded progressively closer. I guessed he'd discovered the stone steps, perhaps even climbed them, then found his way blocked by the platform.

"Good old Mac," Baxter murmured. "He must've remembered to bring a flashlight." Then he raised his voice and shouted. "You'll have to go 'round by the root cellar entrance I told you about. We're tied up here. Can't work the pulleys to let you in this way."

That was when I thought of the rope I'd seen dangling inside the cave entrance on my earlier trip to the island - so long ago, it seemed, though it had been only a matter of weeks. I felt convinced I knew now why the rope was where it was, knew that it had not just gotten hung up by chance.

"Wait! Don't go! There's another way to get in," I screamed, thinking Mac was likely already leaving the cave, surprising myself with the high pitch and loud volume of my voice - not to mention the panicky sound. When there was no reply from the other side of the platform, I screeched, "Are you still there? Can you hear me?"

"Yes," Mac said in a normal voice, which, though muffled, sounded so close at hand that I felt foolish about having shouted - well, bellowed. I recalled then what Baxter had told me about Mac being a man of few words. No kidding! I thought.

Lowering my voice, I explained about the cord hanging inside the cave entrance - "just to the right as you come in," I added. "I think if you pull on it you'll lower the platform."

No sound came from the other side of the platform while Baxter and I waited breathlessly. I could feel Baxter's tenseness now. No more cheery quips. No comments at all.

And then we saw the platform sink, only to rise again with Mac planted firmly on it, looking his usual unflappable self. Without comment, he stepped off the plywood deck, drew out his knife and cut our bonds as if doing this was an everyday occurrence, as commonplace as freeing a snagged line.

-36-

Mac looked around, saying nothing, then said matter-of-factly, "We'd better get out of here. You can tell me about what happened later."

"No," said Baxter, "not till we get what we came for."

I couldn't believe my ears. I'd lost all interest in the papers: I wanted out of this prison - right away. I kept imagining that Brooks and Gordy might have turned back. I told Baxter that but he didn't seem to hear me. Without even glancing at Mac or me, he turned his back on us and felt behind the lamp in the wall niche. Apparently he didn't find the button I'd pressed because the next moment he inquired, "Where'd you say that wall safe was, Angela? Is this the right place?" And without waiting for an answer, he asked, "How'd you get into it?"

It was Mac, not Baxter, who saw my need for reassurance.

"It's O.K., Angela," he said. "I don't like these closed-in places either. Like to be out where I can see what's what. But fact is, we've got time to spare. Can't get off till then, and they can't come in. Tide'll be down below the rocks now. Just made it in myself. Only the mud flats showing." He doled out his words carefully, but he had said enough to ease the tension I was feeling.

I nodded, letting him know I understood. "You can't get across those mud flats, exposed at the tide's lowest ebb, even if it looks like you could walk over them easily. Strangers have tried. Mud's too slippery to stand up on, and where you can stand, you're likely to sink to your knees, maybe up to your eyebrows where a patch of quicksand could suck you down. There are all sorts of old stories about fellows getting swallowed up, buried alive, or drowned when the tide came in and they couldn't move. That was way back when people walked places a lot more than they do now. My granddad used to tell us about way back then."

Despite Mac's reassurances, I still wanted to get outside, breathe the fresh air, see what was what, so it was reluctantly that I turned my attention to opening the wall safe. I continued to feel nauseous. I did not feel so ill as before, but I was still uncomfortable.

When the stone slid back revealing the hole, both Mac and Baxter looked suitably impressed. They appeared surprised too, despite knowing what to expect.

At this juncture, apparently concerned about the shortage of time, Baxter reached in quickly and brought out an armload of the ancient papers and set them down carefully on the table, just as I had when I'd discovered them. Despite his care, more crisp, brown fragments wafted down to the cave floor.

Without turning around he spoke to Mac. "How 'bout putting these in that box I brought for them?" He nodded to the aluminum strongbox which still lay open on the floor where Brooks had abandoned it after finding it empty.

"No time to photograph these now, "Baxter said. "Have to do it once we've got'em aboard. I'm just going to make sure I've got everything out of here."

Mac did as Baxter requested, moving the crumbling papers deftly and carefully while Baxter stood on his toes and reached deep down into the vault. The repository was obviously larger than I had thought. Baxter's long arms extended farther then mine and he hastily extracted a bundle of papers which I had missed.

When Baxter had emptied the wall safe, I asked him which way out we'd take, assuming that now he would be as eager as I was to leave the cave. But he still wasn't attending to me.

"Well, that was quick," he said with satisfaction. "Now for a look behind this wall of boxes. See what's in the other cave before we leave. How 'bout shining your flashlight in there, Mac."

*   *   *

What we saw in that inner cave surprised us all. I suppose I'd expected contemporary contraband. Drugs seemed most likely. Or maybe, I'd thought, Brooks and company were merely warehousing more cigarettes. Booze - hard liquor - was the third possibility which came to mind. Given the immense difference between prices in some states and those in Canada, liquor seemed not unlikely.

And booze it was. The surprise wasn't in the commodity itself but in the brands and the age of the liquor.

This inner cave apparently held a huge selection of hard liquor - *spiritous liquors* - a phrase Baxter's great-grandfather had used frequently in his jottings in both logs and letters. The bottles were carefully packed in crates.

When Baxter and Mac had pried slats off several of these crates, we were amazed to note the dates - all before 1842. The elegance of the bottles and the care with which the labels had been printed also bespoke an earlier age. Here I guessed was a fortune - the wherewithal to stock a good many connoisseurs' cellars and liquor cabinets.

Did hard liquor spoil? I didn't think so. From what I'd picked up - mostly in books - I'd gathered that the passing of time generally increased the value and potability of the best scotch and other *spiritous liquors.*

But it was Baxter who came up with the most amazing find of all - the discovery that the crates were all stamped with an unusual insignia which he recognized instantly. It was a stylized and miniaturized stamp of two of his great-grandfather's ships, the *Angelina II* and *III*.

These consignments of liquor - there must have been three or four at least, Baxter guessed looking around and sounding tremendously excited - had apparently been cargoes salvaged from several of his great-grandfather's later voyages. Neither the *Angelina II* nor *III* had lasted long. Baxter said he'd have to check the time frame again when things settled down. But he knew for a certainty that it was the original *Angelina* which had had a long life. The other two had been unlucky.

"So," Baxter announced, "I'd say all these represent a considerable fortune ..., and, since they have come from the holds of two of the *Angelina*s, I suppose I can lay claim to them - however they came to be here. No wonder Brooks and Gordy were so uptight about our intrusion. The cigarettes they've stashed here are worth a lot, apart from being incriminating, but this cache of spirits is in a different league altogether. Flogging this liquor could make them big-time entrepreneurs. How to do it and get away with it was, of course, their problem. But with the right story - *his* great-grandfather as sea captain, for instance - I imagine Brooks could sell this alcoholic treasure trove. Maybe legally. Maybe not....

"But what I don't understand, though," Baxter continued after a pause, "is why Brooks bothered to break into my house, wanting clues about more loot. If you can believe Brooks' story.... Greed, I suppose.

"Well, if and when the courts allow us to sell this liquor and keep a percentage of the profits, we'll split the money three ways," Baxter said then, thinking aloud. "We have proof that it belongs to me. So if we are permitted to sell this treasure, we'll all be comfortable - more than comfortable - for the rest of our lives."

"Before we all get too carried away, there's the small matter of getting the booze out of here - not to mention ourselves," Mac interjected. "The rest of our lives won't be long if we don't leave now. We've spent too long here already. Tide's on its way in."

I hoped Mac had brought us back to our senses in time. I couldn't wait to get out of the trap we were in. The treasure wasn't that important to me: it wasn't as if I'd grown up with the expectation of being rich.

As we picked up our few belongings and Baxter glommed onto his aluminum strong box, preparatory to leaving, I thought about Mac's clipped and ironic comments. They had surprised me. They seemed more typical of Baxter than Mac. However, now that I'd seen more of Mac, I could better understand why Baxter and he were such fast friends. Their thoughts circulated in similar channels. The big difference was that Baxter was more educated and articulate than Mac and that he liked to pontificate about his favorite subjects which, as far as I knew, Mac did not.

-37-

It was just as well Mac had his head so firmly screwed on. Fortunate too that his life was so closely geared to the ebb and flow of the tides on this bay that he scarcely needed to keep his eye on the water's retreat from the shore or encroachment on it to know what was what.

But what I'd found especially amazing was Mac's ability to *hear* the movement of the sea at times when really no sound was audible to most other human ears. There's nothing wrong with Baxter's ears, yet he said he might just as well be deaf when Mac heard the sea's reverberations inside his head. In fact, because Mac was so attuned to these apparently inaudible sea tones, Baxter had dubbed him Beethoven one evening when we were all kidding around at his place. I don't think Mac got the allusion, but, typically, he hadn't asked for an explanation.

Anyway, it was this sixth sense of Mac's - combined with his good sense - which saved us. He'd been right: we hadn't had a moment to lose.

Speculating that the trap door might be too heavy to push up from inside, we had opted to let ourselves down on the platform to the lower cave and walk out along the shore to our dinghy. Crouched on this outsized dumb waiter, I thought of all the household paraphernalia my grandmother had regularly lowered to the basement and raised from it on her much smaller and more orthodox version of the same invention - and smiled, in spite of the danger we were in, at the image I had of the horror and exasperation she would have manifest if she could have seen me caught up in what I supposed she would have considered a ridiculous situation.

The lower cave was still dry when we stepped off the platform. But when we walked out onto the shale beach, the water was only about four feet away and coming in fast, its progress accelerated by a strengthened onshore wind. Clearly, covering the distance between the cave mouth and the inner crescent beach in time would be a nip and tuck undertaking.

Spray had already dampened the shale so that it was slippery. Trying to keep one's footing was made more difficult by the slant of the beach - almost a 45 degree angle. It was like walking along a steep slate roof in the rain, I thought as I edged along, keeping a most precarious balance. I felt my way along the base of the cliff, keeping as close as possible to the sheer wall. But there was no help here, no vegetation to cling to. And if the worst came to the worst, the cliff face was absolutely impossible to scale. The wall was perpendicular and there were no footholds .

Mac reached safety first. I suppose he expected us to be right behind him. But when he turned to look, he could see that both Baxter and I were in difficulty.

Mac did something then that most people couldn't have done. Wouldn't have managed to pull off either. He turned around and came back for us.

He didn't have far to go to reach Baxter. Probably about 15 feet. I watched him grab Baxter as he slipped - but before he fell - and pull him to safety with apparent ease, like a child pulling a float in a shallow pool.

Reaching me was more difficult. The water was higher by then. Almost up to my waist. But Mac didn't hesitate.

I'd stopped about five feet from the spot where Baxter had slipped, unable to keep my footing either. When Mac reached me I was panicky. I thought death inevitable.

"Give me your hand, Angela," Mac shouted over the rising water and wind.

I reached out unquestioningly, like a child. He grabbed my hand firmly in his huge paw and hauled me quickly through the water.

I don't know how he kept his footing. All those years on slippery and angled decks, I supposed. Just before we reached the safety of the sandy crescent beach I could feel the insidious sucking of the undertow.

-38-

Getting back to the *Black Angel* was another nip and tuck proposition. Because of all we'd been through in the preceding hours, the undertaking was more trying than it would otherwise have been.

I felt at the time that the elements were going out of their way to thwart us - the tide rising so fast that we barely reached the dinghy. It was already afloat. Just. Rain was beginning.

Even after we had climbed aboard the tiny craft, we had trouble reaching the *Black Angel*. With wind and tide against us, the thirty yards or so separating us from the sailboat seemed more like half a mile. That we reached her at all was, I still think, a wonder. Another fifteen minutes and I don't believe we'd have made it.

Even when we were alongside the *Black Angel* our worries weren't exactly over. Given the swell on the Bay and feeling as I did, I couldn't imagine how I could manage the climb up onto that huge hulk.

Why, I thought, crossly, did Baxter have to do everything on such a monumental scale? Why did he have to own a forty-five foot schooner? Surely a thirty-foot Tancook replica would have served his purposes.

Chilled from the wind blowing through my soaked jeans and sweater, I couldn't stop shaking. I noted almost objectively, though, and with surprise, that my nausea had passed. I would have been cheered about that if my hands and feet hadn't felt so numb. How was I going to cling to the rope ladder, let alone ascend it?

Baxter looked the way I felt. Terrible. A pale, bluish-white.

Only Mac looked and seemed normal, capable of dealing with such a difficult situation - or at least giving it a good try. Glancing from Baxter to me, he took charge, sending Baxter up the ladder first, while he steadied the swaying ropes as best he could until Baxter was part way up.

After some slithering around on the bottom rungs, and several partial dunkings as the schooner wallowed in the deepening gullies between the waves, Baxter made it to the top. To my surprise, he pulled himself over the side onto the deck without much apparent difficulty. Perhaps, I thought then, there was hope for me. Faint hope, I added privately.

No more time for reflection. Mac was already urging me onto the ladder. When I reached out tentatively, he gave me a boost and then shouted to me not to worry, that he'd come up right behind me. If I slipped, his wind-borne voice assured me, he'd be there to catch me.

I knew that, truth to tell, he probably wouldn't be able to do that. If I let go it would depend how and where I fell. But I wanted to believe him - to psych myself up to that "willing suspension of disbelief for the moment" which my poetry professor had kept referring to, not always in connection with Coleridge either.

But like Mac, that professor had given me the confidence I'd needed to cope with a frightening situation. As my advisor, he'd been at my thesis defence. Just before the defence began, he'd taken me aside and told me that if I broke down - and I suppose I looked as if I might - he'd take over for me. Although I knew deep down that the powers-that-be likely wouldn't tolerate his doing that, his offer to go out on a limb for me had sustained me. And I had held up. Adrenalin had flowed and I'd come through that trial with flying colors, everyone had said. My professor's assurance had made all the difference.

And so, with Mac behind me, I somehow managed to scale that ladder. Baxter helped me over the side. I lay flat on the deck for a couple of seconds, alarmed by its extreme slant, terrified now that I was going to be tipped overboard.

It was Mac again who encouraged me to carry on and I crawled over to the cabin hatch when the slant of the deck seemed to permit my moving. Baxter opened the hatch and I climbed down the companionway into what I thought was the most luxurious accommodation I had ever seen. The cabin looked just as it had the day Baxter had given me a tour of the schooner. Then I had thought it exceptionally elegant. But after the series of ordeals we'd undergone that day, it seemed like perfection indeed.

*   *   *

A change of clothing, a hot toddy and some of Janet's sandwiches made us all feel somewhat better. But only Mac seemed none the worse for our adventure. He looked ruddy and handsome, his navy-blue eyes bright in his tanned face.

I was glad I couldn't see myself. I felt pinched and shivery still, despite the warmth of the cabin. Probably, I thought, I was still pale, except for my nose which felt burning red. However, I was alive, and content to have survived that day's multiple perils. Who cared how I looked! I thought. Not I.

The bluish tinge to Baxter's skin disappeared slowly, but a waxy pallor remained. He looked as if he needed a doctor.

-39-

We couldn't take Baxter to the doctor and we didn't set sail and disappear from the vicinity of the island. In fact, we didn't do any of the things which a spur-of-the-moment decision would have indicated as appropriate under the circumstances. Mac suggested that we stay put. "At least till we get our bearings," he said. He intimated that cutting and running mightn't be the best course under the circumstances. He told Baxter and me that we should sleep on it. "You can't do anything - even think straight ... particularly think straight ... -" he corrected himself, "without at least a couple hours sleep. Get your forty winks in now when you can. You both need them after all you've been through."

I glanced at Mac and wondered why he didn't figure he needed those forty winks too. But he appeared to be fine - not at all used up, the way Baxter looked and I felt.

"I'll stand watch till dark," he went on. "The wind should've died down by then. We can make plans after you've slept."

To my surprise, Mac carried on talking, explaining. He was

much more voluble than I would have expected. I supposed that, normally, in Baxter's company he couldn't get a word in edgeways - and I'd always seen him with Baxter. I realized then that there was a lot more to Mac than I had thought.

"I don't expect those fellers back right away. You know, your Brooks and Gordy. They'll have had more than enough of their Zodiac in this weather. All that bouncing 'round on their butts, soaked by the spray. No fun at all.

"Our worries start when that twenty-four foot Whaler turns up - you know, the boat their sidekick's supposed to bring in here tomorrow night," Mac explained when he saw me looking vague. "Wasn't it tomorrow night you said you overheard Brooks and Gordy say the other guy was supposed to turn up?" he added, looking suddenly doubtful that he'd got our story right.

I nodded and said I hadn't realized that their larger boat was a Whaler. I was about to ask Mac how he knew and then remembered he'd seen their boat up close last summer, the day he'd waited for Baxter to explore the island. But all I had remembered from that relayed account was that Mac had seen a powerful pleasure craft hovering around the entrance to the cove. A Boston Whaler, with its double hull and amazing maneuverability under most conditions was more than just another expensive power boat. The Atlantic Coast Guard would vouch for that.

* * *

The marine forecaster's voice woke me up.

"Winds decreasing at nightfall. Fog overnight and in the early morning hours along the Fundy coast. Overnight temperatures 8 to 10 degrees. Clearing tomorrow about noon. Increasing winds in late afternoon, gusting to ..." Mac had turned off the radio.

That the forecaster was right about the winds dropping by nightfall was my first conscious reaction as I looked around the cabin and remembered the day's events. Same day still? I supposed it was. Hard to believe!

The schooner was rocking gently now, no longer tossing and pitching as it had been when we came aboard and when I'd fallen asleep.

Mac was lying on a bunk on the opposite side of the cabin, hands behind his head, apparently staring at the ceiling. He had lit one of the kerosene lamps in a wall bracket and the soft light gave the cabin an even more alluring aura than the steely daylight which had filtered in when we had come aboard.

How many hours ago was that? I wondered. Impossible to tell. It was dark outside, but it could still be early evening, I thought. I remembered the heavily overcast sky, the beginning rain, when we had left the island.... Now fog, according to the weather man.

I lay still, pleased with the peacefulness, reluctant to speak, and even more reluctant to participate in the imminent decision-making.

So it was Baxter who spoke up first. I'd thought he was still asleep, but he sounded wide awake and surprisingly chipper.

"Well, what's our next move, crew?"

"Captain's s'pposed to tell *us*!" Mac answered promptly.

We all laughed.

-40-

We decided to stay put till the next evening.

At first I'd been all for fleeing rather than standing our ground. But, as Baxter pointed out - at length - Brooks and Co. would be after us. We knew too much: had seen too much.

"Do you want to spend the rest of your days on the run, always looking over your shoulder?" he asked. "And where to go?"

"So," I said then, panic-stricken, "Let's call the Mounties, alert the Coast Guard. They'll be here with bells on to catch Brooks and his boys when they turn up here tomorrow night."

"Um," said Baxter noncommitally.

"Can't do," Mac said quickly. "You should realize, Angela, how many people could intercept that call - Brooks, Gordy and the other guy, whatever-his-name-is, included."

"Yes, I suppose you're right," I agreed reluctantly. "And so, what do you propose? What's our plan of action? ... If we sit here we won't even surprise them: the *Black Angel* isn't exactly invisible. And just how do we defend ourselves against their guns - the latest, I'll bet...? Roll out the cannons?"

I'd gotten carried away, and, when I paused for breath, I looked from Baxter to Mac. I could see that Baxter was collecting his thoughts, preparatory, I felt sure, to launching into a long, theoretical explanation.

He hadn't smiled at my quip about the cannons. Perhaps he hadn't heard it. I waited for him to begin, and looked over at Mac who winked at me. He knew all the signs too. Could see that Baxter was about to lay out a plan - at length.

Baxter looked hugely better than he had when we'd last come aboard. The waxy hue which had worried me earlier had disappeared. He was still pale, particularly by comparison with Mac, who sat next to him and across from me at our conference table. But then, I reminded myself, almost anyone would look pale alongside Mac.

* * *

"This is the way I see things," Baxter began. "When Brooks and his boys come back - likely in the Whaler, and perhaps towing the Zodiac - they'll expect to see the *Black Angel* where she was when they left. Remember, they don't know we left Mac aboard.

"As soon as they see the schooner anchored in the same location, they'll suppose you and I, Angela, are still tied up in the cave and that they can proceed as they wish - without any special precautions. Then, I'd think, they'd probably anchor offshore and go in in the Zodiac to deal with us - and who knows what else.... What do you think?" He turned to Mac and then to me and we both nodded, waiting for Baxter to continue.

"We'll have a short time to act then. We'll board the Whaler, and you, Angela, since you're used to power boats and not at all used to cannons," he smiled at me wickedly, "can take it back to our fisherman's wharf and call the constabulary.

"Meanwhile, we'll have turned the tables on Brooks and Co.

Imagine! They'll be trapped on the island - depending on where they leave the Zodiac and the state of the tide. And even if they try to get off in the Zodiac, we'll have them covered. Yes, Angela, with the cannons. Fire a shot over their bows if necessary, in old-fashioned privateer fashion." Baxter laughed. He sounded and looked boyish and exuberant. He was obviously having a good time.

-41-

But as my Celtic grandmother was fond of saying - quoting Robbie Burns, who she had always claimed was "the next best thing to Irish": "The best laid schemes o' mice an' men gang aft a-gley."

Baxter's plan for marooning Brooks and Co. on the island and capturing their Whaler didn't work out at all as we had hoped. However, as my grandmother also used to remark frequently, "ignorance is bliss." So, imagining we had the situation pretty much under control, we settled down to make the most of our twenty-four hour wait.

As he had promised, Baxter cooked us a couple of wonderful meals. Since he's such a perfectionist, I guessed he wouldn't be content with just whipping up a quick snack that first evening. Still I thought that, after all we'd been through, he wouldn't feel up to making his usual elaborate preparations. I was wrong. He had sprung back amazingly after his few hours' sleep and seemed to enjoy the undertaking, obviously considering it a challenge to see what he could make out of the dried and canned food he had so carefully chosen and stashed away, months previously, for an emergency which he must then have believed would never really occur.

* * *

Although we took turns standing watch that night - an unnecessary precaution, as it turned out - we all got our eight hours sleep. And, after breakfast the next morning, felt surprisingly fit, ready to turn our attention to Baxter's great-grandfather's papers.

"We'd better get what we can out of them now," Baxter said. "You never know, something in them may have a bearing on our present situation." Then, after a pause, he continued thoughtfully, "This whole business has been such a strange mix of past and present, hasn't it? I can't imagine life ever being quite the same again. Sifting through these fragments from the past alters one's perspective," he went on as he settled down to photographing the crumbling papers we had just retrieved.

I didn't say so then - both because I didn't want to offend Baxter and because I could hardly wait to take another look at the logs - but I felt like telling him I thought he should begin adjusting his perspective from the past to the present. The recent incidents had only intensified his already extraordinarily strong focus on the past, which I had always thought unhealthy. For instance, I still couldn't really fathom the depths of the promptings which had urged him to have the *Black Angel* constructed so meticulously after the pattern of the mantlepiece *Angelina.* He had had her built just before I moved here to the Bay, so I had not been aware of the undertaking then. And of course Baxter had pretty much kept her under wraps since, except for the odd excursions he and Mac had taken on her in fair weather.

-42-

Mac gave up trying to decipher the log book Baxter had handed him.

"I'm no handwriting expert," he said. "I can't do this. Trying to find out what that old geezer had to say just isn't my bag - though I expect I'd have found him just fine if I could've talked to him.

"While you two persevere I'm gonna throw a line over the side. Catch us a fish or two for dinner.... Better have our main meal at noon today so we're all set for visitors later on. Can't show them any sign of life aboard. So I'll cook up my catch while you fellers get on with your reading. At suppertime Baxter can whip us up a snack out of the leftovers.

Actually, even Baxter didn't do much reading - only the odd sentence or set of figures which he could pick out without too much difficulty. Some of these he jotted down, others he read out to me. Chiefly though, he was intent on photographing the crumbling brown documents before they became completely indecipherable.

It was clear to Baxter and to me as well that none of his great-grandfather's papers would yield up their secrets - if secrets they held - without a lot of painstaking scrutiny. Neither of us blamed Mac for giving up on them. Apart from it not being the right time or place, the prospect of reading just a few lines was daunting, even for a person whose focus was on such matters.

Still, I was surprised when, after several hours of poring over the log I had started on earlier, I found I began to grow accustomed to the looped and curled writing, unravelling its knitted pattern so that I became familiar with the formation of each letter - each *stitch*, as it were. Nevertheless, I wished I were a handwriting expert or could call on one - someone who could tell me about this man's character. I've heard that a lot of people believe in the accuracy of such analysis. I wonder, though, whether it's in the same class as palm and tea-leaf readings.

Anyway, without access to any such expert, I had to glean what I could on my own and fared better than I would have expected. The captain's tone was matter-of-fact, his records consisting of page after page of notations about tides, wind and temperatures, the loading and unloading of cargoes, encounters in port and at sea.

As I read on, I could see that the possibility of being diverted onto the rocks by wreckers was only one of a host of hazards the captain faced. It was, however, not one of the disasters you could expect routinely, like most of the others he recorded.

He wrote of iced rigging and slippery decks in mid-winter; of rescuing shipwrecked sailors from swamped vessels; of crew members who tried to jump ship in ports along the way and who were, it seemed, invariably found and returned to the ship in chains; of other men returning from shore leave on time but incubating diseases - mostly syphilis. He recorded the success - or lack of success of the mate-turned-doctor, in treating these cases which mostly flared up in the same men after each stay in port. He wrote of warning these men repeatedly, and eventually dismissing them when they were too sick to work.

I began to wonder why anyone had persevered in the seafaring life in those 'good old days'. So much for the romance of the sea! I thought to myself.

The captain, however, had seemed to take all these difficulties in his stride. Only the shipboard presence of his expectant wife and two-year-old on several voyages had appeared to get him down.

He saw them as creatures too vulnerable to be exposed to the difficulties he faced daily at sea and in most ports. As I read, I found myself agreeing with him.

Yet, absorbing as portions of the captain's accounts of his voyages were, I found no suggestion that they held any of the sort of information Brooks was seeking. This log, was, of course, only one of two I had found in the wall safe. I realized I wouldn't have time to read the other one, or the diary, before carrying out our evening's plan.

It was, however, just as I was about to close the log and put it aside that I noticed a pocket inside the back cover which had not caught my attention previously. The pocket had, I thought, likely been meant for a map or chart, but it no longer held anything so bulky. When I felt inside, there were only three slim envelopes. Drawing them out I looked at the handwriting. It was easily read and addressed in a bold, but I guessed, feminine hand, to the good captain.

-43-

The letters were love letters to Baxter's great-grandfather and signed by Angelina. Spanish must have been the writer's first language. Though the letter was in English, the syntax and tone were not those of a native speaker.

The address Angelina gave was in Buenos Aires. Her tone was passionate and pleading. And although portions of the letters sounded trite and stylized because of the era in which they were written, by and large, there was a directness and immediacy - a sincerity and original-ity about the whole - which transcended time and grammar. The lan-guage was vibrant and the references so personal that I felt embar-rassed to be reading the letters, despite the long years which had passed since they had been written.

There was no mistaking her message. She was begging Baxter's great-grandfather - "my darling and adorable Charlie," as she referred to him at the beginning - to come and take her away with him.

"One day soon," she wrote, "you will be the captain of a great ship - like the one you told me about. You will call her the *Angelina* after me and we will sail in her to all corners of the earth. I shall always go with you. Never will we be parted...."

Angelina's observations, however, were practical as well as passionate. She proposed buying the vessel which was to bear her name with jewels she had apparently just inherited and she was urging her lover to hurry with the schooner's construction, advising him that, because of this windfall, there was no longer any need to postpone their union.

"Now you do not need to wait till you are this great and rich captain for some big company. No need to wait and save, I tell you. If you do not come for me now, my heart will break.

"My grandmother is recently dead. The stones she left me - nearly all set in gold and silver - are more than enough to build the *Angelina* and buy her first cargo. What matter that we are but eighteen? You are a man who is already at sea five years. And I am a woman since two years when we first met."

* * *

I interrupted Baxter's photographing to tell him the gist of the letters. He looked at me thoughtfully and then said, "Ummmm, they explain certain things about the past then. In my teens I came across an unposted letter my great-grandfather had written to this Angelina. The envelope was sealed and I opened it thinking that it had been stuck by the dampness rather than intentionally. This seemed to be the case because the letter was unfinished.

"It must have been an answer to these letters," Baxter went on speculatively. "In the fragment of the letter I read, my great-grandfather told Angelina that he couldn't take the jewels she had inherited from her grandmother to build his schooner. He said he had to earn the money himself. He stated that he thought he had found a way and hoped he would not be long in coming for her. He called her *my black angel*. That's of course where I got the name for this schooner. Even though I had her built as much like the mantelpiece *Angelina* as possible, I thought it would be bad luck to have another. Only the first of that name was lucky. The other two foundered after very few voyages."

-44-

As we had expected, the Boston Whaler appeared about half an hour before the turn of the tide. Brooks and both his henchmen seemed to be aboard. They had the Zodiac in tow.

Mac made these observations discretely, since it was so crucial to our plan that the *Black Angel* appear untenanted. Peering through one of the cannon slots near the stern, he reported that Brooks and Co. had paid no particular attention to the *Black Angel*, seemingly intent on anchoring and going ashore quickly.

The wind was rising again and we guessed they were eager to conclude their business in the cave and be off again before the weather worsened. I broke into a lather just thinking about the *business* these men were intent on - and of the picture they must have in their minds' eye of Baxter and me tied to the rings in the cave.

Perhaps because Brooks and his associates saw no reason to expect anything to have changed since they had left the island, they had apparently decided that only one of them should go ashore. Mac reported that Gordy set off alone in the Zodiac and seemed headed for the bar in the inner bay, not for the cave mouth. We guessed that he planned to enter the cave by the trap door in the briar patch, dispose of Baxter and myself quickly, perhaps torture us for more information first, and then return to the Whaler before the tide receded.

His job would have to be done quickly. I shuddered involuntarily, wishing myself miles away from the island and the present prospect and wondering what we were going to do now that two men were on the Whaler and the third unlikely to be absent for long. Our plan was not going to work.

Boarding the Whaler no longer seemed possible. It was still daylight. And with the rising wind and waves we would need to use the motor on our dinghy. If Brooks and Co. didn't see us coming, they would hear us. We needed to come up with a new scheme - quickly.

-45-

There was no time to lose. We had to act at once. No chance for elaborate planning now.

As soon as Gordy discovered our escape from the cave and reported it to Brooks, those two and the young fellow they employed to run the Whaler were bound to take the offensive. If Gordy could communicate with the Whaler from the cave by two-way radio - which seemed likely - we had a very short time indeed to come up with a plan.

Since boarding the Whaler was now out of the question, cutting and running appeared to be the only alternative - not that we had a chance of outrunning the Whaler, or, it seemed, of outmaneuvering her either. There was, for instance, the small matter of hoisting sails before we could get seriously underway and, given the Whaler's two power-ful motors and her incredible maneuverability, I couldn't imagine how we could get away.

Anyway, we had to try. These weren't only dangerous men - but dangerous men with everything to lose if we were successful in escaping, disclosing their hideaway and bringing about their capture. But it would take a miracle for us to manage any of these feats.

Our best hope was that the ever-increasing wind would prevent Brooks and his sidekick from hearing our frantic activity aboard the *Black Angel*. It did not, of course, interfere with their seeing her sails unfurling.

We were just moving away when the Whaler's occupants fired on us - rapid machine gun bursts apparently directed at our rigging. That Brooks and his sidekick hit nothing on the *Black Angel* must have been due chiefly to the wild action of the waves which precipitated out-of-control antics in both vessels - particularly ours which had just descended into a deep trough when the firing began.

In response to the volleys from the Whaler, Baxter rolled out the cannons and began firing, moving methodically and unflappably down the deck from one to another. This was an extraordinary feat, considering the wild behavior of the schooner and Baxter's unfamiliarity with the actual - as opposed to the theoretical - practice of this antiquated form of gunnery. One moment the *Black Angel* gave every indication that she would descend bow first into the next monstrous wave; the succeeding instant, as another wave raced towards the stern, it was apparent she would meet her end by being swamped. Yet to my amazement, neither of these things happened and Baxter continued to keep his footing. He seemed as unperturbed as he had in his own kitchen the night of Jim's party. I myself hung on to the guardrail for dear life, terrified of being swept overboard.

Baxter appeared to be aiming to frighten Brooks and Co. rather than to sink their craft. The balls fell short, but had the effect of silencing the machine guns. Our adversaries were obviously amazed and had stopped to evaluate their position.

They knew and we knew that once in close to our hull, the advantage, in more moderate seas, would have been theirs. Getting in there, however, without Baxter lobbing a cannon ball into their cockpit was a problem no matter what the weather. Then I realized they would wait for us to tack and then maneuver their boat into position away from the range of our cannon. After that they would move in for the kill.

Meanwhile, under Mac's expert guidance - and with me as obedient deck hand - the *Black Angel* began to glide away from the Whaler. We were sailing wing and wing, and of course the wind was much more advantageous to us than to Brooks and Co. I was beginning to think we might yet stand a chance of getting away, when I realized that Brooks and the young fellow at the tiller were following us at an evenly calculated distance, waiting, sharklike, for their chance to move in. They did not seem to be having any difficulty with the Whaler. She was skimming the waves beautifully. It was with difficulty that I took my eyes off her. When I did, I looked ahead and saw the most horrifying sight of my life.

"Out of the frying pan and into the fire," as I imagined Gram would have remarked if she'd been aboard. We were headed for the wild churning water between the islands. From the deck of the *Black Angel*, this passage looked much as it had from the hill on the island when I had been marooned there during the earlier storm.

A near certain death trap for any vessel, I'd thought then. But close up and about to enter the swirling currents, our vessel's destruction seemed absolutely sure - and imminent. I saw that we were riding on the rim of a violent whirlpool which appeared to be extending its circumference as I stared over the side in horrified and fascinated amazement.

*   *   *

I've read that, when confronted with a cataclysmic death, many people see their whole lives pass rapidly before their eyes. I can't pretend that happened to me as we hovered on the rim of the whirlpool.

Instead, the two things which flashed vividly through my mind just then had happened to other people. The first and clearest image was indeed only fictional. Not typical I'm sure. As Gram had announced to my mother when I was about thirteen - prophetically as usual: "All that reading Angela does is going to leave its mark. I'm concerned by times that it's going to be a substitute for the real world - what's actually going on around her, you know."

So it was that, for an instant, I saw in my mind's eye our being pulled into the whirlpool - swirling down to a seemingly inescapable doom. My vision, if you want to call it that, was, I can see now, closely based on my recollection of Poe's description of his protagonist's descent into the maelstrom. For an instant I imagined the *Black Angel*'s spiraling disappearance into the vortex.

But in the blink of an eye I was back again on the surface. I don't really have any continuous difficulty separating fiction from fact. Just brief flashes. I knew at once that the dizzying descent I had imagined had not occurred - yet. We were still on the rim and I continued to looked down, transfixed, waiting for the horror I felt was bound to happen.

And as I stood grasping the rail - for what seemed like an eternity, but was obviously a fraction of a second - another image presented itself to my mind's eye. This one was recalled from a remembered conversation.

I was a graduate student in Fredericton. This particular evening I was having supper at the Beaverbrook Hotel with a friend when my date and I overheard an elderly lawyer telling his dinner companion at a nearby table about his swim through the Reversing Falls at Saint John. He'd done it on a dare, he'd said, just after returning from overseas.

He'd made it through, he boasted. Just at the turn of the tide, before the whirlpool formed. He could, he said, feel the beginning of its pull.

Funny, he'd said, to get back safe and sound from the war and then risk getting sucked down to one's death in one's own home town.

"Never gone near the water since," he'd said. "Can't. Looking over the edge like that changes a person."

In response to these remembered words, I again stared intently over the side, understanding now how this man must have felt. But to my amazement the whirlpool was disappearing as I watched. There was still the wild turbulence of the water in the passage between the islands, and we were still flying before the wind - though from one moment to the next, even with the mainsail at half mast, we seemed about to founder. Yet somehow, so far, we had avoided what had seemed a sure and horrible fate.

I looked back, and, as we rode up on a monstrous wave, saw that the whirlpool was still there, though much reduced in circumference. Anyway, it seemed much less frightening from this distance and perspective. Then, before I turned away to reassure myself with the comforting sight of Mac's broad immovable back at the wheel, I saw what looked like a toy boat caught in the now distant vortex. "The Whaler," I gasped our loud.

"That's right, the Whaler," Baxter said, putting his arms around me and holding me tight. I hadn't realized he was so close. "No need to man the cannons any longer," he said. "Not this trip, anyway."

He was soaked through and blue with cold, as I was. For a moment we clung together there in the wind just outside the cabin hatch. Neither of us spoke. How to express our relief at our miraculous escape from the whirlpool and our pursuers, our horror at Brooks and Co.'s fate and our mutual comfort in one another's closeness.

-46-

It was long after midnight when we anchored off the dock below Mac's brother's house. Not wanting to disturb the family - and too exhausted anyway even to contemplate going ashore and climbing up to the house - we slept aboard.

We were awakened next morning about nine by someone hallooing from alongside. George was standing on the deck of his Cape Islander and when Mac and Baxter helped him up on deck, he said he'd been trying to attract our attention for the better part of half an hour.

"Must've been quite a pleasure cruise," he remarked laconically, taking in our bedraggled appearance.

And while Baxter made coffee, Mac gave George an abbreviated - and edited - account of our excursion. He described how we had sailed down the bay and anchored off Sheep Island - though he didn't say why we had waited there so long. He went on to tell how we had come home by way of Bright's Passage, skirting the whirlpool which had been forming there as we passed. He didn't elaborate on the dangers we had skirted, but George was obviously aware of the hazards.

"Crazy buggers," he murmured under his breath. But he didn't ask why we'd opted to return that way, just said to Mac: "You'll go through there once too often. Better forget it. In a boat like this one anyway." He gestured disparagingly, obviously judging the cabin in which we sat too fancy - its appurtenances insufficiently utilitarian for his taste - and assuming that the rest of the vessel was comparably frivolous. "What if the wind had died?" he asked after a brief pause.

Mac didn't reply.

So, I thought to myself, Mac's taking us through that channel had been a calculated risk. He'd done it before. More than once, if George was to be believed. He'd figured he could navigate it. I wondered then if he'd guessed what might happen to our pursuers, men who were so much less familiar with these waters than Mac. I didn't want to ask what had been going through his mind. He mightn't even have been able to tell me. I think Mac operates a lot on intuition - intuition grounded in common sense.

Baxter, putting down the steaming cups of coffee, told George then how we'd seen - or thought we'd seen - another boat sucked down into the whirlpool. "Have to notify the authorities about that," he remarked. Then after a pause, he added, "There appeared to be a man on the island too. He'd never have gotten off during such a wild storm. He might be gone now. He had a Zodiac. He might need some assistance."

Baxter didn't mention that part of this *assistance* would be conveying the man to jail.

-47-

Later that morning a coastguard helicopter landed on Sheep Island. Baxter and I accompanied the pilot and two Mounties. We had warned the authorities that we thought the man on the island might be armed. We didn't tell them why and they didn't ask. They were focused on the turbulence and strong winds. The whirring rotor made talking difficult. They said we could fill them in on the details later.

Baxter and I figured we'd have to show the law enforcers the cave. We assumed Gordy would be holed up there. But as had happened throughout this spring's bizarre events, nothing occurred as anticipated.

As we came down to land on the upper part of the crescent beach, we spotted a Zodiac near shore. The Mounties lost no time in inflating their own craft and retrieving the Zodiac. Gordy's body was strapped inside. It was hard to know how he had perished. His body showed no signs of a violent struggle.

Gordy must have decided to try to get off the island before the storm had blown itself out, and, because of the huge waves, had strapped himself into the boat to avoid being swept overboard. I guessed his flight might have been precipitated by seeing his accomplices vanish into the whirlpool and witnessing our escape. He could have seen these events from the hill above the old farm site - from the place where I had stood watching during the last storm.

But we would never know for certain what Gordy had seen and thought. My conjectures were only that - suppositions.

-48-

Baxter, Mac and I still haven't told anyone about the cave and its contents. Up to now there hasn't been any reason to disclose that secret. The three of us, though, have enjoyed thinking and talking about what's there. So far, we haven't been tempted to do anything about the captain's cache. We're content with what we have and think the treasure we've found might be a fortuitous and extraordinary insurance policy.

Before we get much older, though, we have to figure out how to turn over all those cigarettes to the authorities without showing them the cave. If people knew about the cave, the island would be overrun with visitors.

We didn't have to tell the powers-that-be much about Gordy or Brooks and Co. in the Whaler. We said they'd fired on us off Sheep Island which was how we knew they were armed and dangerous. We also told how the Whaler had followed the *Black Angel* and apparently been swallowed up in the whirlpool. They're still searching for the remains.

All we've learned so far is that the fishplant worker - the one Baxter buys his lobsters from - is worried about her nephew who has disappeared. She said he worked part-time for the fish plant when he was in New Brunswick staying with his mother and part-time on his father's fishing boat when he was in Maine. When Baxter heard about this young fellow's disappearance and his aunt's concern, he remembered why Brooks' younger sidekick had seemed familiar. He'd seen him at the fish plant with his aunt - and several times at his own house when he'd delivered lobsters.

"So that was how that young man knew about the house," Baxter told me later. "And I bet he was the one who took Jim's knife a year ago. When he put the lobsters down on the kitchen table or counter, it wouldn't have been much of a trick to slip the knife into his pocket. No sleight-of-hand involved there."

*   *   *

After all we've been through together, Baxter, Mac and I feel very close. I suppose this closeness is a lot like the bond servicemen under fire sometimes forge with their closest buddies. I can understand now - really understand - how my grandfather felt about the two neighbors who'd saved his life on the Normandy beaches.

Between Baxter and me, though, there is an added dimension to our feelings. These recent hair-raising experiences have made us realize how deeply we care for one another. We've always known that we had a lot in common, that we felt singularly comfortable in the other's presence, but now we realize that we can't imagine living the rest of our lives without one another.

EPILOGUE

Baxter and I didn't have a long engagement. After all, it wasn't as if we'd just met.

The wedding took place a week ago in the little stone church where his parents were married. Our reception, planned by Baxter, but catered by a friend of the woman who helps Baxter choose lobsters for special occasions, was held in Baxter's house. Though the food and drink were laid out in the dining room, most of the guests soon moved into the garden, lured outside by the early summer freshness, the shining new leaves, the perfume of lilacs, the banks of multicolored lupins.

We spent our honeymoon on the *Black Angel* and on the island. Today we have returned to Baxter's house, which is where we are going to live. Like Baxter, I think it's pretty much a perfect place.

ABOUT THE AUTHOR

Allison Mitcham is the author of a number of successful books. Several have been on best-seller lists. In 1994 she received British Columbia's Lieutenant Governor's award for *Taku*. Mitcham is professor emeritus of English at the Université de Moncton where she taught graduate and undergraduate literature courses for twenty years before retiring and devoting herself exclusively to writing. She has published 28 books in the past 30 years, as well as scores of poems and articles. Several books have been on Maritime best-seller lists.

Allison Mitcham